I0623272

BATTLEGROUND EARTH

GERRY GRIFFITHS

SEVERED PRESS
HOBART TASMANIA

BATTLEGROUND EARTH

Copyright © 2018 Gerry Griffiths
Copyright © 2018 by Severed Press

WWW.SEVEREDPRESS.COM

All rights reserved. No part of this book may be
reproduced or transmitted in any form or by any
electronic or mechanical means, including
photocopying, recording or by any information and
retrieval system, without the written permission of
the publisher and author, except where permitted by law.
This novel is a work of fiction. Names,
characters, places and incidents are the product of
the author's imagination, or are used fictitiously.
Any resemblance to actual events, locales or persons,
living or dead, is purely coincidental.

ISBN: 978-1-925711-65-3

All rights reserved.

DEDICATION

For Genene

1

It had been 157 days since the crew on the International Space Station had any contact with Ground Control or anyone on Earth for that matter; and now Flight Engineer Cass Freeman was the lone survivor on the habitable artificial satellite that was soon to become uninhabitable.

That tranquil feeling she'd once experienced drifting around the planet like a leaf spinning endlessly in a mountain stream had changed drastically to tumbling in a clothes drier filled with rocks.

Every piece of external equipment on the ISS had been damaged or destroyed passing through the asteroid belt, which for some unexplainable reason had attached itself to Earth's orbital ring and refused to leave, much like a blood-bloated tick on a dog.

Before the last science officer had suffocated due to an airlock breach, she'd alluded to a theory that the denser asteroids were acting as a cheese grater, shredding the 3,000 manmade satellites as they passed through the belt.

Cass gazed out of a window on the cupola, the observation dome that the crew used for watching spacewalks and other activities with an out of this world view. Right now all she could see was a sea of space junk floating by; crushed motor housings, shattered solar panels, and mangled antennas.

The tiny living organisms on the other side of the pitted glass looked like something from a bad cold left on a sneeze guard at a salad bar.

The ISS was completing its pass over the dark side of the planet. Areas that had been dense cities were pitch black. She wondered if they would ever restore power.

Another chunk of space rock fell out of orbit and streaked down through the atmosphere. A twisted weather satellite tumbled earthward.

The alien life forms shimmered as an aspheric sliver of sun shone on the glass.

Cass hugged herself and shivered even though she was wearing her long-sleeved jumpsuit and gloves. It was cold as a tomb and soon the life support system would fail.

All her life she had dreamed of becoming an astronaut and making her family proud, and here she was on her maiden voyage. Now she wondered if any of them were even alive. Something terrible was happening down there, and there was nothing she could do about it as she traveled 17,500 miles per hour 250 miles above the planet like a forgotten message in a bottle.

She gazed down at the Northern Hemisphere and the Great Plains. A wispy layer of white cloud cover parted slowly above the flat wheat-colored landscape.

A large mass was moving easterly.

"What the hell is going on down there?" she screamed.

But no one heard her.

Not even the things clinging to the other side of the glass.

2

Twenty-three M1 Abrams of the 41st Armored Calvary Tank Brigade rumbled across the broad expanse of flatland in a single row almost a quarter-mile wide. Each armored vehicle was spaced fifty feet apart from the next, ample room for the lower section of the tank to complete a 360-degree pivot while the turret remained stationary, never once taking its sights off its intended target.

All gun muzzles pointed in the direction of the perspective enemy steadily catching up, giving the appearance that the tanks were retreating in reverse when in reality, it was the turrets that were facing backward.

Engines roared at a cruising speed of 30 miles per hour; steel tracks tore up the lumpy ground and left prairie dog pancakes.

Ryan Rafferty had only been in for five months and was already Gunners Mate Private First Class and the mechanic on a four-man crew of a sixty-two-ton, four-million-dollar piece of ass-kicking machinery with enough firepower to take down a small army.

Thanks to the shit storm and accelerated boot camp training, worldwide military recruitment was at an all-time high. Fighting for freedom was a thing of the past. The real badge of courage was getting in the trenches defending the human race from extinction.

Standing waist high in the turret's open hatch with the wind buffeting his back, Ryan grabbed both handles on his .50 caliber machinegun and glanced to his right at the other gunners jostling in their tanks, getting their kidneys handed to them as the armored vehicles pounded across the rough open terrain.

He turned, eyes glued on the horizon for the first sign of the enemy. He couldn't help thinking about his family and how everyone had been affected by what was being called an alien invasion.

His stepfather, Frank Travis, said it was more like Mother Nature getting dumped on her head. He had joined a coalition of entomologists and other scientists striving to eliminate the global threat along with Celeste Starr and her associates at the Astronomical Consortium desperately tracking down the meteorite impact sites.

The last time he had heard from his mom, she was heading up the Nor-Cal Militia in a region of California, which had suffered heavy casualties throughout the past few months. He worried about his sister, Ally, a triage volunteer, and missed his little brother, Dillon. They were all living in the Nor-Cal survivor camp. Maybe someday, this would all be over and they could be reunited as a family again.

Rumors were rampant about gargantuan bark beetles devouring the woodlands and the rainforests all over the world, and if they continued at the rate they were going, there wouldn't be a tree left standing in a year's time and the planet's oxygen supply would be depleted.

Bye-bye, Earth.

Ryan was damned if he was going to hand the planet over to a bunch of bugs.

"Hoppers!" a voice boomed in the headset inside his helmet.

He stared out over the grassland and saw a two-mile-wide locust swarm come into view. Even at this distance, he could tell the nomadic grasshoppers were as big as station wagons. It was like a yellow wave rolling over the prairie.

Devouring everything in its path.

The horde took flight and descended on the tanks.

"Give 'em hell boys!"

Twenty-three .50 caliber machineguns opened fire, obliterating the herbivorous insects. The result looked like yellow graffiti being shot out of a leaf blower. But for each hopper annihilated, there was another to take its place.

Ryan swiveled his weapon and knocked half a dozen out of the air. He heard one of the gunners scream. Some of the tanks were completely engulfed by hoppers.

Two of the Abrams broke ranks, careening into each other.

A giant grasshopper chomped on a gunner's helmet and ripped him out of the hatch.

Every tank unleashed its main and secondary armament: M68 rifled guns, smoothbore cannons, and 10,000-round M240 machineguns.

Ryan watched in horror as one of the tanks covered with hoppers swung the barrel of its cannon and fired at the tank next to it. The armored vehicle exploded. Most of the tanks' drivers were operating blind because the tank commanders couldn't give instructions with the view ports smeared with insect entrails. Gunners left as the only eyes on the road.

Two F-18 Super Hornets swooped down from the clouds. The lead jet dropped two bombs and laid out a long fiery swath of napalm that ignited hundreds of hoppers into crispy critters.

The second bomber came in for a pass. A massive wall of locusts rose in the plane's path. The twin engines sputtered as the turbines choked on the bug guts clogging the vanes. The pilot catapulted out seconds before the aircraft nosed into the ground and went up in a blazing plume of black smoke.

"Rafferty, button it up!" Ryan immediately obeyed his tank commander and dropped down, closing the hatch behind him. He squeezed into the tight quarters and manned the gunner position. He looked at the screen on the thermal viewer, but there were too many images to target.

So they waited until the locust swarm was gone.

They'd lost four tanks that day and sixteen crewmembers, not counting the eight gunners killed—men who died in the defense of their planet.

An hour later, Ryan was back in the open hatch manning his .50 caliber machinegun as the convoy of tanks rolled up to the command base surrounded by a twelve-foot tall solar-powered electrical fence and heavily-armed gun towers.

He smiled as his tank passed under the banner he and a few of his buddies had stenciled and hung over the entrance, which read: **WELCOME TO THE NEXT WORLD**

His tank filed into the compound and eventually split away from the procession along with the others and headed to its designated solar shade cover where he would perform his maintenance duties and the rest of the crew would ready the Abrams for its next mission. Their military tent was erected next to the shelter. He was bone-tired and was looking forward to some much-needed bunk time.

As soon as the tank was under the concealment, the rumbling Honeywell turbine engine winded down and turned off.

Ryan climbed out of the hatch. He slid down on the side skirt, which was covered with bug guts like the rest of the tank and stepped cautiously along the hull so as not to slip and fall. He leaned out, grabbed the cannon barrel with both hands, and swung down to the ground.

A military transport raced in through the main gate and came to a screeching halt a few feet from the commissary. The tailgate dropped down. Young recruits jumped out and got in formation. Ryan counted twenty. Not one of them looked any older than him.

"Rafferty!" a voice called out.

Ryan turned and saw the post's administrative clerk approaching. "Yes?"

"Commander sent me to get you."

"Do you have any idea why?"

"Best hear it from him."

Ryan didn't like the sound of that. His heart began to race. Was it bad news?

"All right," he said and followed the military clerk across the compound.

When they reached the command tent, the clerk motioned for Ryan to wait outside while the man ducked between the flaps of the command tent. A few seconds later, the clerk pulled back the canvas opening. "The commander will see you."

The post commander looked up from his desk when Ryan came in and snapped to attention with a crisp salute. The officer saluted back. "At ease, Rafferty."

"You wanted to see me, sir?" Ryan asked, placing his right hand down smartly beside his pant leg.

"That's right." The commander gazed down at the open folder on his desk. "You like being in the Forty-first?"

"Sir?"

The commander looked up and studied Ryan over his reading glasses.

"Very much, sir!"

"Well, I'm afraid I have some bad news."

Ryan began to sway on his feet. He'd been right. He braced himself for the worst.

"You've been reassigned."

He hadn't realized but he'd been holding his breath, waiting to hear that his mother or his sister or little brother were dead. He exhaled the pent-up air. "Where to, sir, if I might ask?"

"A unit operating in San Francisco. North Bay. I take it you're familiar with the area?"

"Yes, sir," Ryan beamed.

"Go pack your gear. A transport will be taking you to the airbase within the hour and Godspeed."

3

Frank Travis drove the black four-wheel-drive Chevrolet Suburban into the vacant parking lot of the Muir Woods National Monument Park. The trip up the coastal highway had been foggy and treacherous, the mist even thicker in the surrounding forest of giant redwoods.

"I used to bring Ryan and Ally here before Dillon was born," Wanda Rafferty-Travis commented, sitting in the front passenger seat. Seemed like an eternity ago, her oldest son and daughter now in their early twenties and her youngest boy almost nine.

She looked down and smiled at Winston, curled by her boots on the floor mat.

The canine had been on her lap for part of the trip but had grown bored staring out the side window and had gone to sleep at her feet, which was fine by Wanda as her muscular fifty-pound pet was a bit much for a lap dog. The white English bull terrier was wide-awake now that the Suburban had stopped. He pushed onto his haunches and stared up at her with his tiny triangular eyes set high in his conical snout. She reached down and scratched behind his ear.

"Nice to see a place untouched by all the madness," Crandall Green said, sitting in the backseat next to his wife, Shelly. He craned his neck and gazed up through the window. "I can't even see the treetops."

"If I remember correctly from a past tour, sequoias can get to be over 250 feet tall," Wanda said.

"That's almost as tall as the Statue of Liberty," Shelly said. Whenever she wasn't out assisting the North Bay Militia, she was back at their home base at San Francisco's Fort Mason, helping to teach school to the many children. Shelly had grown to be close friends with Wanda, so it was not surprising that Dillon Rafferty was one of her favorite students.

"We better get ready. The Eco-Marines should be here any minute," Frank said, checking his wind-up wristwatch. He opened his door and got out. Wanda and the Greens stepped out of the vehicle. Everyone was dressed for the rugged outdoors: heavy waterproof jackets, jeans, hiking boots, and were all wearing side arms.

Winston leaped out and canvassed the parking lot.

The morning sun was blocked by the thick timber and dense fog, but the haze would gradually burn off as the day progressed.

Frank walked around to the back and opened the lift back. He reached into the cargo bay. He handed his wife a Remington pump shotgun and an ammo belt of 12-guage cartridges. Crandall and Shelly preferred to carry 8-shot Ithaca Stakeouts with short barrels and handgrips. Frank grabbed his Mossberg 500 fighting shotgun.

Frank and Crandall wore sheathed machetes on their belts while Wanda and Shelly opted for lighter-weight weapons and carried survival knives.

"Which one do you want?" Frank asked Crandall and held up two crude-looking weapons.

"I think I'll go with the bolt gun," Crandall replied. Frank handed the big fireman the modified spring-loaded captive bolt gun, mounted on the end of a three-foot extension pole, and had a sling so it could be worn across a person's back. Crandall strapped the bovine killer over his shoulder.

Frank grabbed the 18-inch aluminum collapsible shaft that could extend to six feet long and had a carbon steel spearhead at the end designed for swift penetration and easy removal for repetitive stabbings. He slipped a protective hard-plastic cover over the sharp tip and stuffed the compact weapon inside a daypack, which he slipped on.

Wanda saw Winston sitting regally by a trail next to a brown wooden sign with large white lettering: *No Pets*.

"Aren't you the funny boy," she said. She coaxed him over with a friendly wave.

Winston immediately sprang to his feet, raced over, and stood guard by her side.

"This isn't like them to be late," Frank said, consulting his watch again. He closed up the back of the Suburban.

"Maybe they met up with some trouble," Crandall said.

"They better get here soon," Wanda said, "or we're going to miss our window."

Winston barked loudly.

A diesel engine could be heard approaching in the fog.

4

The gray military vehicle appeared out of the mist like an apparition and headed into the parking lot. A large winch was mounted on the front bumper of the huge truck. The all-terrain front tires were massive, five-feet in diameter. A side gas tank with a step-up was under the driver's door, another tank on the other side. There were two sets of passenger doors behind the main cab.

Instead of traditional rear wheels, there was a trailer with dual-axle wheels attached behind the passenger section of the truck like a railroad car coupled to the back of a locomotive. The trailer was completely covered with a steel meshed screen, high enough that a person could stand upright inside.

Frank could hear metal canisters clanging together inside the trailer as the truck pulled up to a stop.

The doors swung open and military-looking personnel quickly jumped out.

"Had a bit of engine trouble on the bridge," Eco-Marine Squad Leader Max Simms yelled out as he climbed down from the driver's side.

"I don't have to remind you we're under the clock," Frank said, pointing to his wristwatch.

"I know. Come on, everybody. Shake a leg!"

Frank recognized the other members of Max's six-person squad as they had all worked together numerous times. He watched as the specialists gathered their gear and collected their weapons. Ace McElroy and Vince Rocklin were already up in the caged trailer. Ace was the armory specialist and always wore a flamethrower pack. Vince was the grenadier and ordinance specialist and handled the explosives.

Julie Brown had been an entomologist student of Frank's at UC Davis and was now utilizing that knowledge as a threat assessment specialist. The other woman on the team was Denise Washington. She was a preservation specialist and it was her job to make sure the team stayed within the perimeters of the mission and kept landscape destruction to a minimum while eradicating the enemy.

The sixth person on the team was their medic, Johnny Horn.

Each squad member wore a helmet, camouflaged jacket and trousers, and combat boots. Julie, Denise, and even Johnny, were armed with Colt M16s and 9mm Glock pistols. Even though they looked like enlisted personnel in the military, Eco-Marine squads were actually made up of civilians that had received cram courses in weapon training and combat skills, and were led by a member that had served in the armed forces.

Max had been a staff sergeant in the U.S. Marines for nearly twenty-years and had been contemplating retiring from active duty when the planet became overrun.

"I want everyone to put on vests," Max said. He looked over at Frank. "You guys better wear yours, too."

"Good idea," Frank replied. He turned and opened the lift on the Suburban. He grabbed four orange safety vests with yellow stripes that road construction crews would normally wear so that they would be visible to motorists. In this case, it was a preventative measure from being accidentally shot in the event there was an encounter and they were attacked in the dense forest.

Everyone mustered at the trailhead.

Max was holding a 40mm six-shot grenade launcher.

Vince wore an orange vest that held three rows of grenades in the front. A row of eight stretched across his stomach then another eight above that with four on his chest: twenty in all. The ones above his belt were chemical grenades with highly concentrated pesticide used sparingly as the dispersion was so toxic and sometimes difficult to contain, especially during windy conditions. The other twelve cylinders were high explosive, fragmentation, or stun grenades.

He knew exactly which type of bomb was in each pouch and could pick the right one with his eyes closed, and depending on the situation, could grab a hand grenade, yank the pin, and pitch it like an all-star in a split second.

Vince had also strapped on a drop-leg shotgun holster with a short-barrel pump shotgun with a pistol grip so that his hands would be free at all times. He often joked that he liked wearing the rig because it made him look like the Steve McQueen character Josh Randall in the old-time TV western *Wanted Dead or Alive* even though the actor's modified rifle had been a Winchester lever-action.

Ace stood out from the group as he was wearing a silver fire proximity suit and had the hood clipped in his belt next to his striker tool. He wore a twin canister pack on his back. A hose ran from a regulator to the nozzle gun in his asbestos-gloved hands.

Each of the squad, except for Ace, had hard plastic gas masks hooked to their belts that resembled the helmet worn by Darth Vader. When fastened over the head, a battery-operated power pack on their belts would activate a small blower and generate a steady stream of air into their masks, which was more comfortable than wearing the old-type rubber gas masks that were often difficult to breathe in.

"You want us to take the lead?" Max asked Frank.

"Sure." Frank reached in his jacket pocket, took out a hand-held GPS receiver, and switched it on. He looked at the blank screen. "Nothing yet."

Wanda was holding a small notebook. She flipped through the pages then stopped. She showed the page to Frank. "Is this it?"

Frank checked the coordinates on the page. "Yeah, that's it." He looked over at the squad leader. "Let's go down this way. I should be picking up a signal pretty soon."

Max led the group down the wide dirt-packed trail bordered on both sides by split rail fencing.

Frank carried the Mossberg in the crook of his arm with the muzzle pointed at the ground like a pheasant hunter and started down the trail, keeping one eye on the device in his hand.

Wanda walked right behind him, Winston close at her side.

Crandall and Shelly followed, taking up the rear.

Everyone was on high alert, knowing that the slightest inattentive moment would result in certain death.

5

After hiking for more than a mile, Max raised his right hand and clamped it into a fist, signaling for everyone to stop. He pointed to something in the trees to his left. Julie stepped over the railing to take a look. She trod cautiously on the spongy carpet of pine needles and through the waist-high ferns, staring down the gun barrel of her M16 with the stock pressed against her shoulder.

Crandall hopped over the fencing. He moved quickly across the forest floor.

"Is it one of ours?" Max called out, keeping his voice low.

Julie approached the twisted mound of metal embedded in the ground. Crandall joined her and they inspected the wreckage, which was the size of a crumbled refrigerator.

"I don't see any markings," Crandall said.

"Scorched off during reentry." Julie turned and looked at Max. "We can't tell."

"Any idea what type?" Frank asked Julie.

"There's no way of knowing."

Since the invasion, satellites—or pieces of them—had been dropping out of the sky and plummeting to Earth. Space junk and meteorites were continuously raining down unexpectedly.

Which was one reason Frank was forced to wait for the exact moment that at least three still-functioning Global Positioning System satellites were able to form a trilateration and pinpoint a specific location, a window that only presented itself twice a day. Lately, the signals had been getting progressively weaker, and he knew eventually, the transmissions would cease altogether.

The Astronomical Consortium had been collecting data and tracking the meteorite impact sites, which were passed on so Eco-Marine search teams could be dispatched to those locations. There was no real way of knowing how many groups were scouring the globe. Frank thought it might be in the thousands though it was difficult to say with any degree of accuracy as it was estimated that half of the world's population had been wiped off the face of the planet within the past six months.

Frank stared down at his GPS receiver. "I'm picking up a signal!" He looked to Wanda.

She brought the notebook over and they compared the latitude and longitude that appeared on the screen with that written on the page. "We need to keep heading north up the trail," Wanda said.

"Keep going! We're almost there," Frank yelled up to Max.

Julie and Crandall came back and stepped over the split rail fence.

The patrol had gone maybe a quarter mile when they came across a giant banana slug, which confirmed they were going in the right direction. The enormous slimy, green gastropod was eight feet long. Dried leaves and soil clung to its mucous-covered body as it moved slowly across the decomposed matter on the ground. It looked like a humongous chili relleno stuffed with a log of Monterey Jack cheese.

Frank stepped over the railing to approach the animal. The slug's two-foot long tentacles, which had been fully erect, instantly shrunk into its head once it sensed Frank was walking towards it. Even though the detritivore was intricate in the natural cycle of creating humus soil, Frank feared a creature this size could do more harm than good as it's life span could reach up to seven years.

Rather than take a chance, Frank pulled out his machete. He stood for a moment, pondering his actions before driving the tip of the blade deep into the pneumostome, which was the respiratory opening. He cut around inside the right side of the body and perforated the slug's single lung. The slug reacted immediately and began to shrivel, even changing in color to an insipid brown.

He put his machete back in the sheath and went back to join the others.

Wanda could see the downtrodden look on his face. "You hated doing that, I can tell."

"Well, it wasn't like it was an immediate threat."

"Maybe not yet," Wanda said and gave him a tender smile.

Frank knew she was right and loved her for understanding his pain of having to destroy such a magnificent specimen, which under any other circumstance would have been any entomologist's dream of discovering; but not anymore.

He glanced at his GPS. "Shouldn't be far now."

They kept hiking and had gone the distance of a football field when Frank realized that the GPS receiver wasn't going to be of any further use because the screen had gone blank. He raised the device in his hand

and called out, "I've lost the signal!" then slipped the device in his pocket.

"All right, everyone fan out!" Max hollered. He continued up the trail with his six-shot grenade launcher at the ready.

Ace and Johnny stayed on the path. Denise and Vince hopped over the fence and combed the forest on the right while Julie went to the left. Crandall and Shelly stepped over the barrier and spread out behind Julie.

"You want to split up?" Frank asked Wanda.

"Not really. Let's get ahead of Ace and Johnny."

Even though Ace was a strong young man, he was lugging the heavy oxyacetylene tanks on his back. Frank could tell by the armory specialist's gait that his legs were beginning to feel the burn from the long hike.

Frank and Wanda picked up the pace and quickly overtook the two men in front of them. Winston was happy to be in the lead and galloped ahead.

The forest was beginning to thicken as they reached a bend. Frank looked in both directions but didn't see any of the others even though they should have stood out like a sore thumb, wearing their bright-colored safety vests.

"Over here!" a voice yelled out in the woods. It was Crandall.

Max vaulted over the split rail fence and charged through the trees.

"Winston, come!" Wanda yelled to the English bull terrier. The dog spun around and ran back. Wanda and Frank had no sooner cleared the fence than Winston bounded over right behind them.

Denise and Vince crossed over the pathway and headed in the direction of the voice that hollered again, "This way!"

Everyone gathered around Crandall who was staring down at chunks of what had been a large rock that had split apart and was ten feet at the bottom of a crater twenty-feet in diameter.

"This can't be good," Wanda said, when she saw the fragmented rock.

"I better take a look," Frank said. He passed his shotgun to Wanda then reached inside his coat pocket and took out a rectangular magnifying glass equipped with a small light.

"Be careful," Wanda said.

"I should be okay. So far, they haven't been too interested in us," Frank said.

"Yeah, well you never know," Wanda said. "Just don't take any chances."

He glanced around the group and saw the concerned looks. Even Winston was agitated and was letting out a low rumbling growl as he glared down at the bottom of the crater.

Frank scooted down the dirt slope. As always, the first thing he did was scout the surrounding ground for insects. He used the toe of his boot and kicked up the loose debris, exposing some earthworms and a few shellback snails, which didn't concern him.

Something caught his eye by his feet so he bent down and brushed away the loose soil.

"What is it?" Wanda asked from above.

Frank looked up and showed the bug in his hand. "Redwood bark beetle."

"Should have known," Crandall said.

The beetle was an inch long and had six legs. Its head, antenna, and mandibles were black and were partially hidden under a dark brown shell that covered almost half of its body. The abdomen portion was a lighter brown. In large numbers, bark beetles could have a devastating effect on woodlands as they would bore deep inside tree trunks and lay their eggs. Later the young would choose their own path and eat their way out, eventually killing the tree.

Frank dropped the beetle on the ground and squashed it under his boot.

He decided to inspect the largest section of rock. Turning on the light on the magnifying glass, he got down on his knees, and peered through the lens to examine the surface of the meteorite.

Tiny organisms in the porous rock shrank away from the light. Their bodies were gray and translucent. They had tiny grappling-like claws at the ends of their squid-like tentacles that they used to anchor themselves to the rock.

Frank stood and climbed out of the crater. He looked over at Ace. "It's all yours."

Ace nodded, removed his hood from his belt, and slipped it on over his head.

Vince stood behind the man in the fire-retardant suit and opened the valves on the top of the tanks strapped to Ace's back.

Ace hobbled down into the crater and managed to get to the bottom without falling. He grabbed the striker tool off his belt and twisted the knob on the gun nozzle.

A stream of gas came out the end. Ace clicked the striker and caused a spark that ignited the gas into a flame. He adjusted the intensity until the blue flame became white.

Frank watched from above. He was glad to have been part of the research team that had learned how to destroy the invading life forms that at first seemed to be indestructible. Especially when they could survive frigid temperatures in space of -454 degree Fahrenheit, and then endure 2,400 degree Fahrenheit heat riding in a meteorite traveling 30 miles per second as it hurled through Earth's atmosphere. Not to mention the impact of the crash.

The answer had been extreme heat—6,330 degrees Fahrenheit—that could only be achieved by combining oxygen and acetylene.

Ace attacked each portion of rock with his torch, and after nearly fifteen minutes, melted them down to nothing. He turned off the nozzle and slowly climbed out of the pit.

"Nice job," Frank said after Ace removed his hood. The young man's hair was sopping wet and he was sweating profusely like he had just stepped out of a sauna bath.

"It's shitty work but someone's got to do it."

Everyone let out a hearty laugh. Winston joined in and barked.

The bull terrier kept barking, and continued barking, even after the last person stopped laughing.

"Winston, it's okay. You can stop," Wanda said. She knelt and covered his muzzle with her hand to quiet him down.

That's when they heard the pandemonium in the forest.

"Sounds like a damn army," Max said.

6

Sequoia redwoods had few predators, which was why they had survived on the planet for 2,000 years. The tannin in the wood made it unsavory for termites. The trees were almost impervious to fire because of their foot-thick bark that insulated the core, which had very little resin for fuel. Often bark beetles chose to ignore the challenge and moved on to softwood cedars and cypresses.

But not anymore—not when the bark beetles were as big as Volkswagen Karmann Ghia automobiles and weighed over 600 pounds.

It was difficult to get an accurate count of how many there were moving between the thick trees but Frank figured there had to be at least fifty if not more. Each one was extremely dangerous as their powerful mandibles could easily cut a person in two.

The Eco-Marines and Frank's group quickly caught up to the rear of the horde and started attacking the giant beetles.

Julie and Denise opened up with their M16s. Their bullets ripped through three of the giant insects, blasting open their abdomens, and sending green goop splashing against the tree trunks.

Crandall ran alongside one of the beetles and held out his Ithaca. He got close enough and shot it in the head. The beetle dropped to the ground. Shelly was a few feet back, ratcheting her shotgun as she kept up with her husband.

Max spotted four bugs darting into a small clearing. He aimed his grenade launcher and fired off two projectiles. The bombs hit their target and exploded, blowing the giant beetles apart.

Johnny and Vince ran up to a tree that had to be ten feet wide. A beetle was already boring into its trunk and was three feet in. Wearing heavy gloves, the men grabbed the beetle's hind legs and began to pull. "Damn this thing's strong," Johnny yelled over to Vince.

"Keep pulling," Vince shouted. He put his foot on the tree trunk and yanked on the leg, which had sharp barbs.

They keep tugging and finally the beetle fell out onto its back. Vince drew the short-barrel shotgun from the drop holster and fired two rounds into the exposed abdomen. Johnny stepped back as the underbelly ruptured and bug guts flew up.

Wanda ran up on a beetle that had begun chewing its way into the bark of a tree.

She fired her Remington into the creature's thorax, immobilizing it on the spot.

Hearing Winston barking, she turned and saw the dog chase after a beetle. She was about to run after him when Frank yelled out, "Wanda look out!" She'd been distracted watching Winston that she hadn't realized she was standing in the direct path of an approaching bark beetle.

She took a step back as she pulled back the slide to ram another shell in the receiver...and tripped over a log.

The giant beetle opened it jaws and stepped over her, its belly only a foot above Wanda so she was unable to raise the barrel of her gun to shoot. She gazed up into its grotesque mouth as it hovered over her; its menacing jaws ready to close.

Frank advanced with the razor-sharp spear and drove the carbon steel tip through the beetle's head. He released the shaft, grabbed Wanda by the hand, and pulled her out from under the beetle before the monstrosity collapsed to the ground.

"Sorry I took so long. I couldn't chance using the shotgun or I might have hit you," Frank said.

"No need to apologize," Wanda said and got to her feet. "Don't forget your pig sticker."

"Oh, yeah." Frank walked over and pulled out the spear. He quickly retracted it and stuffed it in his backpack. He picked his shotgun off the ground where he had dropped it before saving Wanda.

All around them, they could hear the staccato of rapid machinegun fire and explosives. Frank and Wanda ran toward the gunfire.

Julie, Denise, and Johnny were standing back-to-back firing short three-round bursts up into the trees. Some of the beetles had taken flight and were trying to escape into the canopy. Heavy bodies were crashing down, snapping off tree limbs.

Frank counted seven beetles dead on the ground, and more were dropping.

"Watch out!" Johnny yelled and moved away. Julie dashed toward a tree trunk for cover. Denise wasn't so lucky. A giant beetle came down directly on top of her.

"Oh Jesus," Wanda said as she and Frank ran over.

"Keep firing!" Frank yelled to Johnny and Julie. "We can't let any of them get away!"

The two Eco-Marines pointed their muzzles up at the sky and strafed the treetops.

Frank got down on the ground and tried to look under the fallen beetle to see if he could see Denise. Part of her was visible. The blank expression on her face told him she was dead. Her eyes were open and blood was funneling out of her mouth meaning her internal organs had been crushed and ruptured.

Johnny and Julie emptied their thirty-round clips and paused to reload.

"Everyone, mask up!" Vince yelled from close by.

Frank watched as Johnny and Julie reached for the gas masks on their belts and immediately started putting them on. He looked at Wanda. "We better get the hell out of here."

Wanda glanced around. "Where's Winston?"

"I don't know. We need to go."

"Not without Winston."

"Wanda. Vince is going to use chemical grenades."

"We're far enough away."

Frank felt a breeze and saw the fog around them wisp through the trees. They were only 20 miles away from the Pacific Ocean, so coastal winds were prevalent in the area.

"He sets those off, the gas is going straight for us. Go!" Frank grabbed Wanda by the arm and they started running.

Crandall was standing next to a dead beetle. He was retracting the deadly rod back into the spring mechanism of the bolt gun. He looked up as Frank and Wanda raced towards him.

"Where's Shelly?" Frank shouted.

"I'm not sure," Crandall replied.

"We have to get out of here, they're going to release chemical bombs."

"Shit!" Crandall glanced around the trees. He grabbed his shotgun off the ground and ran after Frank and Wanda.

Frank heard a concussion grenade go off then looked over his shoulder. He could see a yellowish cloud, which meant that Vince had also lobbed at least one chemical grenade. The wind was blowing in their direction.

"Run!" Frank and Wanda ran over to the dirt path and jumped over the split rail fence like a couple of track stars vaulting over a set of hurdles. The ground was flat and solid so they were able to run faster. Crandall wasn't far behind. He was fast for a big man and was catching up.

Wanda almost stumbled but Frank made sure she didn't fall and kept her on her feet.

He glanced over his shoulder again. The fog was burning off. He couldn't see any hint of a yellowish mist.

"I think we're okay," he said, and came to an abrupt halt. Wanda and Crandall stopped running as well.

"I hate it when they use those," Crandall said.

"Vince would only use a chemical grenade as a last resort," Frank said. "The beetles must have massed together. It's the best way. Let's hold up and wait for them."

Twenty minutes later, they saw Max coming down the trail. He was still wearing his Darth Vader gas mask and was carrying Denise's body over his shoulder. The four other Eco-Marines trailed behind. When they saw Frank, they began to remove their breathing apparatus.

Julie's eyes were red from crying and Johnny was walking close by her side with one arm over her shoulder in a consoling manner.

Ace shuffled down the path in his fire-retardant suit with a sullen look on his face.

Vince was carrying Max's grenade launcher.

"Did anyone see my wife?" Crandall asked.

"No," Vince said. He looked to the others. "How about you guys?"

Ace, Julie, and Johnny shook their heads.

"Could somebody please take off my mask?" Max asked.

Vince rushed over and removed the helmet from Max's head.

"Thanks," Max said. He readjusted Denise's body on his shoulder.

"How about Winston?" Wanda said. "Did anyone see our dog?"

Again, the response was no.

Frank put his hand on Wanda's arm. "He'll show up. He always does."

They stayed close together and continued down the path. In less than an hour, they were back at the parking lot. Something very big was lying beside the Suburban.

It was a dead beetle.

Shelly walked out from behind the truck to greet everyone and had a smile on her face until she saw what was draped over Max's shoulder.

"Oh my God. Is that Denise?"

"I'm afraid so," Frank said.

"I'm so sorry."

"What happened here?" Wanda asked, staring at the dead beetle, riddled with bullet holes.

"It tried to get away. I followed it all the way back here."

"Good thing you got it," Wanda said.

"I had help."

"What?"

Shelly turned and pointed inside the truck.

Winston was gazing out the half-opened window, licking the glass.

7

Vince helped Max put Denise in a black body bag. They each took an end and lifted the bag inside the trailer next to the oxyacetylene bottles strapped against the inside wall. Ace took off his twin tanks and fire-retardant suit and placed them in the trailer.

Everyone gathered around in a circle, held hands, and bowed their heads. Max said a few words. Julie ended the impromptu service with a short prayer. And then, as if they were breaking from a huddle, the group dispersed.

Frank, Wanda, and the Greens got in the Suburban while Max and his squad climbed into the transport truck. Max started up the beefy diesel engine and headed out of the parking lot. Frank pulled the Suburban around and followed.

Even though the fog had dissipated somewhat in the forest, it was still thick coming down the road. It wasn't long before they were passing through the streets of Mill Valley. Frank looked out his side window. The town looked deserted even though he knew that there were some people still alive and residing in the community.

He figured they had heard the engines and gone into hiding. Lately, there had been reports of increasing activity of marauders. It wasn't bad enough innocent people had to worry about stepping out their doors and being eaten by some damn mutated bug, they had to be afraid of their own kind hunting them down and killing them.

At first, the role of the militia groups had been to assist the Eco-Marines in eliminating the bug scourge, but human nature being what it was, their duties soon expanded to protecting law-abiding civilians from renegade gangs and looters.

With everyone in survival-mode there was no one willing to watch over the jails or prisons. While some convicts managed to escape—usually the most violent—many inmates had been left in their cells and died horrible deaths. Frank couldn't believe how a civilized society could crumble so fast in only a matter of six months; but it had.

Frank turned onto the onramp and followed the transport as it accelerated onto Highway 1.

"It's really socked in," Wanda said. Normally from this vantage point near Sausalito they should have been able to see the city high-rises of San Francisco just ahead to their left but the fog cover was too thick. It was like driving through a cottony cloud.

Frank quickly lost sight of the taillights on the transport truck's trailer. He switched the headlights on low beam and turned on the windshield wipers. He glanced at the instrument panel to see how fast they were going and reduced his speed.

"I can't see a thing," Wanda said.

"At least we won't have to contend with the toll booths on this side," Crandall said from the backseat, meaning they wouldn't have to stop at the checkpoint before crossing the bridge.

"Maybe we should just pull over and wait for it to clear," Shelly said, stroking the back of Winston's neck as he took a nap on her lap.

"Let's see how it goes," Frank said, determined to keep going. "It should clear up once we get to the other side."

He rolled down his window a notch, letting in a blast of cold ocean air. He decided to slow down even more and let his foot off the gas pedal. That's when he saw a red flare burning up ahead. He pulled the Suburban to the side and stopped.

Frank put the shifter into park and let the engine idle. He opened his door and climbed out. He cupped his hands around his mouth and yelled, "Hello!"

"Over here," Max replied in the fog.

"What's wrong?" Even though Frank could see the glow of the flare, he couldn't see Max or their vehicle.

"The engine up and quit. Ace thinks it's a clogged fuel line. He's working on it."

Frank heard a door open behind him and turned.

"We shouldn't be standing out here exposed," Wanda said. She was carrying both of their shotguns. She handed Frank the Mossberg.

Frank turned and saw Crandall and Shelly's silhouettes in the mist as they had gotten out too. Frank heard something race up to his feet, and looked down. Winston brushed against his pant leg and sat next Wanda. The dog's coat was already damp from the heavy fog.

As they walked toward the flare fizzling on the pavement, they could hear hundreds of seagulls high above, shrieking and flapping their wings.

Wanda looked up and squinted. "How in the world can they see in this fog?"

Frank spotted the back of the trailer. Johnny was standing guard and was pointing his M16 at them.

"It's just us," Frank said, relieved when Johnny lowered his weapon. It was easy to get jumpy in the fog. He certainly didn't want them getting shot by friendly fire. The seagulls got even louder.

As they came around the side of the transport, Frank saw Julie and Vince standing with their automatic rifles by the open hood. Ace was standing on top of the winch on the front bumper, leaning inside the engine compartment.

He came out from under the hood, holding a rubber hose. He put one end to his mouth and blew gunk out the other end. "See, I was right. It was the fuel line," he said with a grin.

"Hey, look," Max said, stepping around the front of the vehicle. "I can see some blue sky."

Frank gazed up. A wind had picked up and was shifting the fog in a southerly direction. He could make out the top of the North Tower, 500 feet up with its two massive cables sloping down and a portion of the suspension cables that held up the six-lane roadway that crossed the one-mile stretch of water.

That's when he saw the birds. "We might have a problem!" Frank yelled.

"Oh my God," Wanda said.

"Everybody stand ready!" Max shouted to his squad.

The seagulls weren't perched on the cables.

They were caught in giant intricate webs.

Some of the gulls were already dead, covered in silk, while the ones alive were flapping their wings and snapping at the sticky webbing with their beaks in an effort to break free. The more they struggled, the more entangled they became. Frank knew he was only seeing a fraction of the snared birds. For all he knew, there could be hundreds more in the fog.

"Hurry up under there," Max yelled to Ace, who was having trouble reconnecting the hose to the fuel line.

"I am, I am!" Ace hollered back from under the hood.

Julie pointed at a shadow up above. "I see one!"

Frank looked up. He should have been horrified but instead he was amazed at the magnificent creature. The orb-weaving spider's body was as big a round as a hot tub and had a head the size of a beach ball. Each time the spiral wheel-shaped web jiggled, the spider would skitter over to the source making it move.

As the fog shifted, Frank saw more spiders scaling down from the network of webs that stretched down from the top of the tower.

"Everybody get back in your vehicles, I've got this," Max yelled. He went around the side of the transport, peered through the collimator gun sight that aligned a dot on his intended target, and fired a single projectile from his six-shot grenade launcher.

There was a loud concussion as a spider exploded fifty feet up above their heads. Parts of the arachnid fell down through the webbing, ripping sections of the rope-thick silk apart. Many of the seagulls were tumbling out of the sticking entrapment and falling—and so were the spiders.

"Look out!" Julie shouted when a giant spider landed on the cab of the transport.

It seemed unharmed as it struggled to get on its feet, slipping on the slick surface of the metal. As the spider rose, its front legs slid down the glass surface of the windshield.

"I'm done," Ace shouted. He reached up, grabbed the front of the hood, and slammed the cover down. He was shocked to see he was face-to-face with the hideous-looking creature, especially when it glared back at him with its eight black-orbed eyes.

Julie jumped on the step-up over the gas tank and opened up with her machinegun. She fired off a second short burst. The high-caliber bullets ripped through the spider's abdomen, causing it to lose its footing. It slid from the hood onto the pavement where Johnny walked up and finished it off with his weapon.

The spring-driven cylinder rotated on the launcher as Max fired two more grenades, killing another spider and further destroying the massive webbing. He opened the driver's door and climbed up inside the transport truck.

Wanda fired her shotgun at a humongous spider climbing down the cable and it plummeted off the bridge. A faint splash could be heard a few seconds later as it landed in the ocean two hundred fifty feet below.

Frank ran over and got in the Suburban. He waited until Wanda and Winston were inside before putting the idling engine into gear. Crandall and Shelly were already in the back.

The fog was clearing and Frank could see roughly a hundred feet in front of the Suburban. The southbound three-lane roadway was covered with dead birds. There were also more than a hundred derelict automobiles that had been pushed to the side to make a path for working vehicles.

He glanced up at the ragged webbing flapping in the wind and knew by tomorrow morning the industrious spiders would have either repaired the damage or engineered an entirely new network of webs. Like the other giant insects that had taken over the planet, the orb-weavers had made their claim to the Golden Gate Bridge. During the day they stayed mostly out of sight, nestled in the sub-structure and girders under the deck but today the overabundance of snared seagulls had been too much of a temptation for them to ignore. The spiders were generally known to come out at night to inventory their webs, spinning their victims in silk cocoons then later returning to suck the hapless corpses dry of all bodily fluids.

Frank was relieved to hear the diesel engine fire up on the transport. The truck shook as it started to roll away in low gear then gradually picked up speed.

He glanced over at Wanda. Winston was sitting on her lap, gazing out the passenger window. She was holding him tight and staring straight ahead. Even though she was a strong woman and had been a sheriff before the invasion, there were times when even she was humbly reminded of the dangers they faced everyday and how easily their lives could be cut short.

Denise Washington had only just joined Max's team and this had been her first outing with the other members, which unfortunately turned out to be her last.

8

Cass propelled herself through the tight confines of the passageway. She had no sense of up or down in the zero gravity and had to be cautious not to strike her head on anything protruding from the bulkheads as she floated about. There were handholds along the way designed to aid the astronauts so they could control their movements, but after some practice living in the weightless environment, she'd mastered the ability to fly and navigate the inside of the space station gracefully like a comic book superhero.

She drifted into the U.S. module, Tranquility, as she desperately needed to use the toilet. Weightlessness and eating only freeze-dried food had done a number on her digestive system, not to mention her nerves frayed being trapped inside a failing craft spinning around the planet.

The toilet compartment was similar to the one used in the Zvezda module as Russian engineers had designed both. She quickly entered the tight quarters and undid the bottom of her jumpsuit. On Earth, going to the bathroom was just a matter of sitting down on the toilet seat and doing one's business. Up in space it was nothing short of being an unglamorous chore.

To urinate, she had to use an oval-shaped cup that sucked her pee down through a hose; for bowel movements, there was a fan-driven suction system on a sit-down toilet that collected her solid waste in micro-perforated bags, and to do either one was a different process. Being able to separate the two urges was often difficult if not impossible to control.

After she was done, she drifted out of the toilet compartment.

A thin plastic bag filled with a small amount of water was attached to the bulkhead, along with a flat white washrag. Cass squirted a single globule of water from the bag's tip. The clear sphere wobbled in front of her face. She quickly captured the droplet on the washrag and cleaned her hands.

Water was the most precious commodity on board—along of course with breathable air—and the most dangerous. If allowed to float freely, a small dabble of water could land on a piece of equipment and cause an electrical fire.

Cass maneuvered over to the shaft opening and returned to the cupola for another look around. The seven windows facing Earth's surface also gave her a view of the other modules and structures that were still attached to the space station; and of course the tiny alien life forms that clung to the outer glass by their tentacles.

Before the asteroids had destroyed major portions of the spacecraft it had been over 350-feet across with wing-like solar panels made up of two four-panel sections on either side that generated electricity. Cass could see from her vantage point that most of the panels had been destroyed or were severely damaged with gaping holes.

The Russian sleeping quarters module, Zvezda was dinged and battered, but the metal hull seemed intact.

She glanced out another window and saw Kibo, the Japanese science lab. The largest module looked like a crushed, aluminum soda can and had become the crypt to three researchers, one being the American science officer. The Canadarm2, the crane used for positioning equipment out in space had been damaged and was missing three of its seven motorized joints, rendering it useless.

Cass stared through the center glass piece of the observation dome at the Russian spacecraft, Soyuz, docked below the connecting module, Zarya.

Zarya had taken a tremendous beating traveling through the asteroid belt. Cass could see the rough outer skin of an asteroid sticking out of the module's hull near the mating coupler, which had blocked the passage to the access hatch to Soyuz. Also, after a system check, she discovered the compartment had a lower oxygen level than normal which might merely be a faulty reading on the gauge or the result of an atmospheric leak.

Which posed a serious problem.

The spacecraft, Soyuz, was the only means of getting off the International Space Station and returning to Earth.

9

Frank followed the military transport through the main entrance and past the gatehouse of Fort Mason, which had once been the San Francisco Port of Embarkation for the U.S. Army years ago before it became part of the Golden Gate National Recreation Area and open to the public for special events.

He remembered Wanda telling him how excited Ryan and Ally had been when they visited the area a couple years back and attended the Walker Stalker Convention that was being hosted at Fort Mason. They'd been able to see some of their favorite stars from the hit zombie TV series *The Walking Dead*. Ryan and Ally had been just as excited to see characters on group panels that had been killed off in earlier episodes and were no longer on the show as well as actors still alive and portraying their roles in the upcoming season.

Everyone on the TV show was always in fear of being attacked by a zombie and turning into one themselves or getting killed by a ruthless, violent person.

Funny how life could imitate art: as now it was giant insects instead of zombies suddenly appearing, and marauding gunmen, attacking people.

So, it seemed fitting that Fort Mason had become the central stronghold for Bay Area survivors.

Four of the whitewashed, red-tiled roofed three-story buildings had been reverted back to barracks to accommodate the influx of civilians wanting to escape the lawlessness that had prevailed over the city.

Every man and woman was trained to fight.

There were 600 members from the Nor-Cal and North Bay Militias, 40 six-person-squad Eco-Marines, and 200 children—many of them orphans—residing on the base.

Frank pulled the Suburban next to Max's big truck and trailer that took up two stalls.

He shut off the engine and everyone piled out. He checked his watch and saw that it was almost five in the afternoon. There were maybe thirty vehicles scattered throughout the parking lot, some military trucks and a few humvees, but mostly civilian cars and pickups. At any given time, there could be up to 200 vehicles on the base but that was a rarity as everyone shared shifts out on patrol both night and day.

"You guys going over to the commissary?" Frank asked Max.

"As soon as we get the truck squared away for the next team. We'll see you in a bit."

"Okay," Frank replied then turned to Wanda. "Hungry?"

"Yes. Dillon should be waiting for us in his classroom."

"We'll get him on the way."

Frank turned to Crandall and Shelly. "How about you two?"

"No, I think we'll head over a little later," Shelly answered for the both of them. "I think we're going to grab a shower." She glanced up at Crandall and gave him a wink, making her husband blush.

The Greens headed toward the entrance door to the barracks in Building C.

Frank and Wanda walked straight ahead in between the loading docks that ran along the lengths of Building C and Building D.

Winston ran ahead of them, knowing the routine by heart. The bull terrier scrambled up the steel stairs that led onto the concrete loading dock. He raced up to a side door and scratched at the wood frame.

"We're coming, hold your horses," Wanda said, letting Frank open the door.

Winston bolted inside and ran off down the hall.

Frank could hear children laughing and playing as he stepped inside. "Sounds like someone's having a good time."

They followed the gaiety and stood outside the classroom door.

Twenty kids were huddled around, giggling while Winston stood on his hind legs, licking Wanda's son's face.

"Hey, quit slobbering me," eight-year-old Dillon protested, wiping away the wet.

"He loves you," Wanda smiled.

"Okay, everyone, class dismissed," a young woman said, who was acting substitute as this was normally Shelly Green's students, but like every able body, it had been her rotation to go out on patrol with Frank's group.

The children kept laughing and filed out of the classroom.

"Feel like some food?" Wanda asked Dillon.

"Can I have chicken nuggets?"

"Do you even know what a nugget is?" Frank asked.

"Ah, yeah. It's a..." Dillon paused to think. "I don't know. What is a nugget?"

"Got me."

"Come on, let's—" but then Wanda stopped when she heard children screaming from out in the hall.

"What the hell?" Frank said. He ran toward the doorway and almost tripped over Winston as the dog bolted out into the corridor.

Many of the children were running back. Frank stepped aside as they crowded back into the classroom.

"What is it?" Wanda asked, stopping a frightened young girl.

"It's a daddy-longlegs!"

"You go inside. We'll handle it."

The girl gave her a brave smile and scampered into the classroom.

"Is this all of them?" Frank asked the substitute teacher.

The woman did a quick headcount. "No, there's two missing."

Frank and Wanda stormed out and raced down the hallway.

The little girl had been wrong. There wasn't one but four spiders creeping down the hall. Their fused-together abdomens and cephalothoraxes were as big as fifty-five gallon drums and were touching the floor. Their gangly legs extended upward almost brushing the ceiling then elbowed downward to the floor.

One of the giant spiders was actually eating off the end of its own leg, as the appendage had grown too long for it to walk properly.

A young boy was holding onto Winston's collar as the dog backed up and barked at the stilt-like creatures scooting across the floor.

"Over here, over here," Wanda yelled to the boy.

As soon as the boy saw Frank and Wanda, he let go of Winston and ran toward them.

"You're safe now. Go to the classroom," Wanda instructed, and the boy did as he was told.

"We're missing one," Wanda said.

"Yeah, I know," Frank replied.

The English bull terrier stopped barking and looked back at Wanda.

"Go find 'em."

Winston turned and ran toward the spiders, keeping close to the wall so that he could sneak under their legs and avoid being bitten.

Even as big as they were, the lanky spiders looked fragile. They had short fangs but were just as deadly because of their enormous size. A single bite would be fatal to a child.

Frank could hear Winston barking farther down the hall.

"I think he found the student," Wanda said.

"Let's go." Frank drew his sidearm. He waltzed up to the first spider and shot it between the eyes—all eight of them. Wanda came up from behind and fired a 12-guage round into the next arachnid, creating a gory mess.

The spider that was gnawing on the end of its leg suddenly realized that it might be in danger and peered up at Frank. He put a bullet in its head and watched it slump to the floor.

Frank and Wanda stepped around the splatter and rounded a corner.

Winston had the last spider by a hind leg, grabbing it between his teeth, and was pulling it away from a scared girl cowering under a stairwell. The daddy-longlegs was trying to turn around to defend itself but was having trouble, stumbling over its own feet.

Wanda shoved the barrel of her shotgun into the spider's ugly face and pulled the trigger. The separated spider parts twitched on the floor then became still.

Frank and Wanda rushed over to the little girl.

"You're okay," Wanda said, kneeling down.

"Did you see that?" the little girl asked. "Dillon's dog saved me."

"Yes, he did." Wanda looked up at Frank and grinned.

Winston went up to the girl with his tail wagging, and licked her hand.

After they had returned the girl back to the classroom, Frank and Wanda took Dillon and Winston and headed over to the Herbst Pavilion. The long, warehouse-like building stretched along Pier 2 and was used for storing supplies and the armory. There was also a triage for the wounded and a crack battlefield-experienced surgical team.

A nearby heliport had been set up for a medevac team in the event a patient had to be transported to one of the few hospitals still operating in and outside the city limits; each hospital heavily guarded by North Bay Militia to prevent thieves and drug addicts from breaking in and stealing life-saving medicines.

They entered through the massive main entrance and quickly found Ally talking with Dr. Gemma Tubbs, lead veterinarian in charge of making sure the livestock in the surrounding areas remained healthy. Tick infestation was a major problem, especially the insects that had ingested the alien life forms and had increased to the size of skillets.

Mutated cow killers were a serious threat, and could get as large as bobcats. The wasps looked like hairy orange ants and would travel in swarms on the ground, attacking the hooves and legs of cattle and horses.

Ally looked over and smiled at Wanda. "Hi, Mom."

Dillon came over and Ally ruffled his hair. She leaned down and patted Winston on the back.

"We were just about to go over to the Festival Pavilion and have something to eat. Want to come?" Wanda asked.

"Sure."

"How was your patrol?" Gemma asked.

"We saved some trees," Frank said.

"Thank God. I've been talking with Ally and she tells me she was studying at UC Davis to become a veterinarian."

"Yes, that's right," Wanda said.

"Well, to be honest, I've been a little short-handed and could really use some help. I talked with Dr. Miner in triage and she said that if it was okay with you, she'd let Ally come and assist me."

"You mean go out in the field?"

"That's right. Of course, we would always have an escort."

"What do you think, Mom? Can I?"

Wanda looked at Frank hoping to get his input.

"It's something she's trained for. I think she should. Given that you have an Eco-Marine team with you or some of our people accompanying you at all times."

"We will," Gemma responded.

"Just promise me you'll be careful out there," Wanda said.

"I promise," Ally replied, and hugged her mother.

"Okay, then."

"Well, now that that's settled, how bout we go eat?" Frank said.

10

Ryan sat in the cabin behind the pilot and copilot of the battle-ready Bell UH-1 Iroquois. The Vietnam War era Huey was one of many reinstated fighting machines taken out of mothballs since the satellites went dark, crippling modern warfare. Even though the chopper was shuttling him to his next assignment and he was a passenger, he was still expected to be an acting member of the flight crew as an emanate attack could happen anytime without warning.

He was sitting on a small bench and had taken on temporary duty as a side gunner behind a 50-caliber belt-fed machinegun, the long barrel pointing out the open side door.

The wind felt good on his face as the whirlybird flew low, hugging the rolling hills at a cruising speed of 125 miles an hour.

Ryan gazed down and saw a black herd marching single file through the rough terrain of manzanita and scrub oaks. The pilot's voice sounded in Ryan's headset that he was going to make a sweep around.

The Huey circled and hovered in position 100 feet above the ground.

Ryan fired the 50-caliber machinegun. Every fifth bullet was a tracer so he could align the magnesium sulfate trail and pinpoint his targets. The deadly barrage tore up the ground, kicking dust into the air. The high-caliber bullets proceeded up the procession ripping through bodies, annihilating the giant harvest ants. From up in the air, they almost looked like normal-sized ants even though Ryan knew they had to be at least eight feet in length. He continued firing, the steady stream of projectiles cutting them in half.

His body shook along with the powerful weapon as though he and the metal were fused together. Brass casings ejected out onto the deck and piled up all around his boots.

Ryan ceased firing. He counted close to twenty dead.

He remembered the adrenaline rush he used to get as a kid, shooting at fake monsters in a video game. This was way, way beyond that. Instead of earning game points, his satisfaction was knowing he had eradicated another mutated horde from the planet.

The pilot gave him the thumbs up and pushed forward on the stick, once again, heading the Huey toward the crimson horizon.

With dusk approaching, the helicopter soared over sprawling suburban neighborhoods on the outskirts of metropolitan areas. Many of the houses were scorched and complete blocks had been burned to the ground due to fractured underground gas pipes that had been ruptured by giant burrowing insects.

The Huey flew over the Benicia refinery surrounded by scores of oil storage tanks. Ryan didn't see any smoke belching out of the stacks and wondered how long it had been since the facility stopped producing petroleum. He could see the channel and counted three oil tankers run aground.

Turning south, the pilot skirted the banks of San Pablo Bay and took them over Richmond. Ryan gazed at the old shipyards below as they passed over what looked equally deserted as every other location he had witnessed from the air.

As they flew over the Richmond-San Rafael Bridge, Ryan could see multiple wrecks and abandoned bumper-to-bumper vehicles that had been there for a long period of time, left by stranded motorists that had to set out on foot in order to cross the span.

Flying low over the choppy waters of the San Francisco Bay, Ryan got his first glimpse of the mayhem. He had heard stories and seen video coverage of the devastation but none of it had really prepared him for what he saw.

The waterway was congested with hundreds of sailboats that had once been moored at the marina but were now either capsized or had gone adrift with their masts snapped off. He saw two cargo container ships that had collided into one another and spilled thousands of twenty-foot long sea vans, most of them floating in the bay.

As it grew dark and they got closer, Ryan could see the cityscape but not many lights. Many of the big power plants in the area had gone off-line when the satellites designed to regulate the energy usage caused the overloaded grids to crash when the meteors destroyed the orbiting computer systems. Without power, the pumping stations throughout the region had shut down and drinkable water was no longer available to businesses and residents.

If that wasn't bad enough, there wasn't any cell phone or Internet services, as most of the communication satellites were no longer operational, which meant that survivors had to rely on alternative methods like CB radios, walkie-talkies, and landline phones.

He gazed past the landing skid and looked for signs of life as the Huey flew through the high-rise canyons of glass and steel.

A group of people was on the rooftop of a tall building. They were all armed with rifles, and looked up when they heard the drone of the Huey overhead. Ryan expected them to wave as they flew by, but instead one of them raised his weapon and aimed up at the helicopter. Ryan pointed the muzzle of the 50-caliber at the rooftop. The man quickly lowered his gun once he saw he was seriously outmatched.

Normally, San Francisco's streets would be bustling with traffic and pedestrians flocking the sidewalks, but not anymore. It was too dangerous to venture out even to scavenge for water, food, and supplies because the city would be crawling with mutated insects and roaming gangs of pillagers.

It was inconceivable to think, that only half a year ago, the population of the Bay Area had been upward of over 8 million people. There was no telling how many had died of thirst or starved to death behind bolted doors rather than face the atrocities outside.

Ryan saw a few vehicles maneuvering between the buildings. It was difficult from this height to tell if they were friendly or hostiles.

It wouldn't be long before the nocturnal predators would be coming out of their hidey-holes in search of food.

"We're setting down," the pilot called out.

Ryan could see a halo of bright lights surrounding the heavily fortified camp and the three piers jutting out into the bay, which had managed to restore power tapping into a still working electrical grid.

He was anxious to celebrate and finally reunite with his mom, sister, and little brother after not seeing them for almost six months.

The Huey came down on the heliport and the engine wound down. Ryan could hear wailing sirens. A combat-ready army of militia and Eco-Marines began to pour out of the nearby barracks to take up defenses.

The happy reunion would have to wait.

Fort Mason was under attack.

11

Frank, Wanda, Ally, and Dillon had just finished eating at the mess hall in Festival Pavilion and were heading to their cottage that had once been an officer's quarters when the sirens began blaring. Winston was trotting beside Wanda. His ears perked up at the irritating sound.

"Ally, take Dillon and Winston over to the hostel," Wanda said, which was the nearest safe place to get them out of harm's way. The hostel was set up for sleeping quarters, recreation rooms, and had a cafeteria and dining room. There were large rooms, which were more ideal for families unlike the barracks that were meant for single individuals or married couples without children who didn't mind living with large groups of people and sleeping in a double bunk.

Floodlights were coming on, lighting up Fort Mason like a football stadium ready for a night game.

They ran to the concrete retainer wall that separated parts of the park. Frank helped Ally up first then Dillon. He lifted Winston and handed the dog up to Ally.

"Hurry!" Frank said.

"And be careful," Wanda added.

"We will," Ally promised and took off with Dillon and Winston. They quickly disappeared in the trees in search of the path that would take them to the hostel.

Frank looked around and saw hundreds of people running to their posts.

A voice came over Wanda's walkie-talkie. "Wanda, this is Crandall, can you hear me?"

Wanda unclipped the two-way radio from her belt and answered, "Yes, Crandall. Do we have a breach?"

"Not exactly. There's a tenement fire behind Bay Street."

"We'll be right there." Wanda clipped her radio back on her belt. Most of the neighborhood was apartment complexes and adjoining two-story single-family houses and had suffered structural damage from past fires. Only a few buildings remained standing with the rest of the areas nothing but rubble and resembling a bombsite.

Frank and Wanda ran parallel with the retaining wall.

Bay Street stretched along the perimeter of one side of Fort Mason at a higher elevation and overlooked the encampment. It was impossible to see anything on the street from below which made it the fort's weakest point of defense.

Frank and Wanda dashed behind a line of fighters positioned at a four-foot tall wall of sandbags stretching halfway across the base.

Fifty feet back was a second perimeter of forty vehicles parked side by side, some humvees and armored personnel carriers commandeered from an abandoned National Guard armory, but mostly pickup trucks that had standup M60 machineguns mounted on the cargo beds that were often used by ragtag rebel fighters. They were all facing the direction of the grassy hillock called Great Meadow that sloped up to Bay Street.

More infantry fighters and armored vehicles were positioned to fend off attacks from the other three sides. Fifteen gunboats were loosely moored at the three piers, ready in the event of a maritime attack.

As an added advantage, 20 mobile cherry pickers were strategically placed about the battlement. The cages were extended twenty feet in the air and were used as lookout platforms. Each guard was armed with a six-barrel rotary M134 minigun that could fire 6,000 rounds per minute.

"We need a bird's eye view," Wanda said to Frank and stopped at the first aerial lift they came to. She rapped on the metal motor housing to get the attention of the lookout up above. The man glanced down and immediately lowered the cage.

Frank removed the safety chain. Wanda climbed aboard then Frank. All four sides of the cage were reinforced with one-inch thick steel plates to deflect low-caliber bullets but was useless against armor-piercing projectiles.

The guard operated the control box and they started up. The lift arm extended as far up as it could go, giving them the best view possible. It also meant that they were sitting ducks to any hostile snipers.

Wanda got on her walkie-talkie. "Turn off the alarms."

A few seconds passed and the sirens went quiet.

"So what are you seeing?" Wanda asked the guard.

"Two blocks back."

"I see it," Frank said. Smoke was funneling out of a broken second floor window of a four-story apartment building. Orange flames belched out of the structure.

"Has there been any activity over there?" Wanda asked.

"I haven't seen anyone," the guard said, "but I did hear a car engine."

"Do you think there's hostiles out there; maybe they set the fire?" Frank said.

"Doesn't make any sense." Wanda watched as the fire licked up the side of the building. "There isn't enough fuel out there for it to spread this way." Bay Street was a natural firebreak, and even if embers did blow down on Fort Mason, most of the buildings had Spanish tiled roofs that would likely protect the structures and prevent them from catching fire.

But on the other hand, there were 200 vehicles with full gasoline tanks, and a fenced area with over 100 fifty-five gallon drums of petroleum and diesel fuel, and a tinderbox of ammunition inside Herbst Pavilion; so it didn't hurt to be vigilant because if all that were to catch fire, it would the most spectacular fireworks show in San Francisco history.

Not to mention that, if Fort Mason were to become a raging inferno, there was only one means of escape—the bay. Even with the 15 gunboats, they'd only be lucky to get a hundred people to safety.

"Jesus, will you look at that!" the guard yelled.

The black mass poured down over the grassy hill like a giant oil spill. It was the largest intrusion Wanda and Frank had seen in a long while. With their bodies pressed together, the cockroaches looked like a single sheet of medieval chainmail armor; each roach being eight feet long.

Everyone behind the sandbags opened up on the invading horde. The gunners in the row of vehicles directly behind fired their weapons. The low-caliber rounds ricocheted off the roaches' hard shells. Only the high-powered bullets were able to punch through, and when they did, white goop shot out of the roaches' bodies.

The downward assault turned into an avalanche as the roaches skittered down the hill, stumbling over their dead, and tumbled down the retainer wall.

The only thing separating the fighters and the onslaught was the sandbags and a thick veil of gun smoke.

Wanda looked down and saw the roaches clambering over the sandbags. She could hear the screams and yelling even with the guard standing next to her, firing his minigun. Instead of retreating, the militia fighters and the Eco-Marines stood their ground and unleashed everything they had.

The roaches that stormed over the barrier were met with strong opposition. Many of the Eco-Marines were armed with long bayonets and were jumping on the backs of the roaches. Even though the roaches' bodies were completely covered with protective plates, there was just enough space between the overlapping shells behind the head to insert a sharp blade, which was enough to sever the ganglia controlling the nervous system and paralyze the creatures.

Only when the fighters were out of ammunition, did they fall back.

"What the hell?" Frank turned and looked up. "Get down!"

They ducked in the cage just as a helicopter swooped over their heads.

Wanda spun around. A moving wall of fire converged onto Great Meadow. The cockroaches taking up the rear were burning alive and had been the reason for the stampede.

The gunner in the helicopter fired down on the flaming insects as the aircraft hovered over the hillside. Each roach killed in the barrage, stumbled, tripping up the bugs racing behind it. Many of them ended up on their backs, smothering the flames, but it didn't save them, as they were already dead.

Wanda glanced down at the battlefield below and saw some of the wounded on the ground lying amongst over a hundred defeated insects. Most of the gunfire had subsided. The gunner in the cage stopped firing.

"You don't think they purposely started that fire to stampede those roaches?" Wanda said. It wasn't the first time the hostiles had tried to attack Fort Mason but it was the first time they had devised a way to use the bugs to their advantage.

"You have to admit, it was pretty ingenious," Frank said.

"And where did this chopper come from?" Wanda asked, as the aircraft banked toward the helipad between one of the barracks and the waterfront.

"Not sure," Frank said. "Let's go find out. I think a 'thank you' may be in order."

The lookout lowered the cage to the ground and let Wanda and Frank out. They hurried across the crowded parking lot, stopping briefly to congratulate small groups as the able-bodied pitched in and helped the wounded over to the triage.

Wanda and Frank reached the helipad and waited for the chopper's engine to shut down. A young man jumped down out of the side door and gave Wanda a big smile.

"Hi, Mom."

12

Even though Cass was weary and desperately wanted to get some sleep, she knew she was wasting her time. It didn't make any difference that she was bundled up in her sleeping bag with her favorite foam pillow and was comfortably strapped in so she wouldn't float out and injure herself because no matter how hard she tried, she just couldn't clear her mind.

Losing sleep worrying about work or something trivial that later ended up resolving itself was one thing, but knowing she had only a few precious days left to live was enough to keep anyone up at night. Or day. It didn't really matter what time it was floating up in space.

Cass undid the strap and unzipped the side of her bag. She wormed her way out of her sleeping bay—slightly bigger than a gym locker—and propelled herself into the Harmony's cylindrical passage through the open hatchway of the berthing port and into the laboratory of the U. S. module, Destiny.

"Hello, Rob. How are things?" she said to the sole occupant. Normally she would love to kid around and joke with the humanoid robot even if the lifeless robonaut would never respond.

Rob was an advanced spin-off version from the Dextrous Robotic Program but hadn't been fully tested as the scientist assembling the robot had been killed before completing his assignment.

From the waist up—Rob was currently without legs, as the limbs hadn't been attached—the robonaut was modeled to look almost human. Its torso and arms were white and covered with a flame retardant material. The abdomen section contained the computer components that controlled all mechanical movements and other functions such as speech and reasoning.

The upper parts of the arms rotated in the shoulder sockets much like a child's doll and could be removed for modifications and repairs. Each mechanical hand was designed like that of a person; a thumb and four fingers with touch sensors on the tips and had a high degree of flexibility and dexterity.

The striking part about Rob was its head, which looked like a brass Power Ranger helmet. There were no facial features, just a dark visor that was a window for four cameras inside the cranium and an aperture below that could have been mistaken for a small mouth but was really a viewer for a depth perception camera.

Without legs, Rob looked like it was wading waist deep in the bulkhead. Rob's battery pack and energy source were tethered separately to the bulkhead.

Cass made her way over to the round 20-inch nadir observation window often used for taking breathtaking photographs of Earth.

Now it was a portal into hell.

As the space station made its sweep over the daylight side of the planet, a dark shadow passed over the glass. Cass watched as the behemoth asteroid—the biggest in the belt—blocked out the sun. She'd been monitoring the planetoid for weeks and had witnessed its destructive force. Just like many of the smaller asteroids, it would only be a matter of time before the massive rock experienced orbital decay and plummeted through the atmosphere.

13

The last few nights, Wade Waters had been keeping watch on his deck, not so much for the great view he had from his home, tucked in the hills a short walking distance from Emerald Lake, but because his neighbor, Jack Stonewall, had spotted looters in the area.

Most of Wade's friends and the people that lived around him had packed up long ago and left to go live in militia encampments where it was said to be safer. But there were those that refused to leave and remained in their homes defending their families and property, much like Wade was doing. Many of them had either been brutally killed by murderous thieves or by the damn mutant bugs. It seemed lately the hills were crawling with them.

He'd slept on and off for maybe a total of two hours, waking up to the tiniest sound which a few months ago might have been a field mouse or rabbit, but not any more, not with those things out there. Usually, it was a nervous bird, hiding and flittering in the branches of the nearby oak by the side of his rustic home, but even they were becoming scarce. Wade couldn't remember the last time he'd heard a whippoorwill or a bluejay.

His back ached from sitting in the redwood patio chair even though it had a padded seat and back. He had his 10-shot Marlin lever action carbine draped across his lap, resting on the wood armrests, and wore a shoulder rig with a Browning nine-millimeter in the holster just inside his heavy coat. It had gotten so cold in the night he had pulled his black watch cap down over his ears.

Looking out beyond the porch railing, he could see parts of Redwood City, what was left of it, and the old salt flats by the bay. The sun was beginning to crest over the easterly mountain range.

Wade picked his rifle up and leaned it against the side of his chair. He pushed himself out of the seat and stood, stretching his arms over his head to straighten out the kinks in his body. A hot cup of coffee sounded good. He could make a pot and surprise Debra before she woke up.

He heard a high-pitched scream from the house. It was his daughter, Amy.

Wade grabbed his rifle and ran across the deck. He opened the sliding glass door, dashing inside.

"Mommy, Mommy!" Amy screamed.

Wade charged down the hallway. Debra was standing outside Amy's bedroom, holding their frightened daughter.

"What is it? What's wrong?" Wade asked.

"There's a spider in my room," Amy said.

"What kind?"

"It was big and black."

"My God, Wade. It could be a black widow," Debra said.

"Did you see it?"

"No. I heard Amy scream and when I came out, she was standing in the hall."

"Okay, you guys stay back," Wade said. "Take Amy into our room."

"Watch yourself," Debra said. She put her arm around Amy, shuffled her into the next room, and shut the door.

Wade raised his rifle and levered a round into the chamber. He nudged the door with the toe of his boot and it swung halfway open. He could see only a portion of the room. Amy's dresser and dollhouse were against one wall along with her toy box. He could see the foot of her small bed, but not the window. Amy had been persistent, complaining her room was too hot and kept insisting her window be left open while she slept. Wade had told her positively no, that there were evil monsters outside.

Obviously he hadn't gotten through to her.

Maybe if he could have shown her the giant waterbugs he'd seen skimming across Emerald Lake, eating the trout and bass, she would have been more receptive and quit nagging him about the damn window.

He pushed the door the rest of the way until it bumped against the wall.

"Wade, you okay out there?" Debra called out from the other room.

"Yeah," he answered. "Quit yelling." He stepped over the threshold. Amy was right. The room was hot. Cold sweat dripped down the inside of his flannel shirt.

He rammed the rifle stock against his shoulder, peered over the sight, and scanned the room with his gun muzzle.

The window *was* open.

Shit.

Then he saw it crawling on the wall over the rainbow and unicorn wallpaper.

Debra had been right.

It was a black widow.

And it was huge.

Wade walked over with his rifle, waited until the spider crept onto the hardwood floor...

And squashed it under his boot.

He closed the window and made sure it was locked. Later he'd nail it shut.

"Okay, it's safe to come out now!"

14

"I should have done this long before now," Jake Reynolds said, standing on the loading platform as more flatbed trucks carrying high stacks of sectioned cyclone fencing pulled in. The North Bay Militia leader gripped his coffee mug in his right hand and took a drink. His left shirtsleeve was folded and pinned to his shoulder.

"Crandall asked around the barracks and put together a crew that used to work construction," Wanda said. "He said the fence will be up by the end of the day. They'll top it off with razor wire."

"How high?" Jake asked.

"Twelve feet. They're also going to run generators at night and electrify the fence."

"That should keep them out."

"Maybe, but it'll slow them down."

"Were you surprised to see your son?" Jake asked, trying his best not to smirk.

"Yes. How in the world did you swing that?"

"Wasn't me. It was that husband of yours."

"Frank got Ryan transferred out here?" Wanda said, astonished.

"Seems he knows how to pull some strings. He never told you?"

"No."

"Guess he wanted it to be a surprise."

"It was a surprise all right."

"Have Crandall keep me posted on their progress," Jake said.

"I'll tell him." Wanda turned and headed across the loading dock. Reaching the top of the steps, she hurried down and walked briskly to a picnic area set up near the entrances to the piers where her family was enjoying an outdoors breakfast.

"Hope you saved something for me." Wanda stepped over the bench attached to the picnic table and sat between Ryan and Frank, who was already pouring a cup of coffee from a thermos.

"Here, it's still hot." Frank placed her mug on the table.

"Thank you, dear." Wanda gave Frank a quick kiss then turned and gave Ryan a peck on the cheek.

"Mom, I'm not twelve," Ryan griped even though it was plain to see he really didn't mind his mother's affection.

"Yeah, kissing's for sissies," Dillon said, sitting across the table next to Ally.

"How about I give you a big whopper?" Wanda said. She reached over the table and puckered her lips.

"Yuck," Dillon said and slid off the bench to hide under the table.

"Get up here, mister," Ally said, pulling her little brother back onto the seat.

"Did you know Ryan has his own tank?" Dillon said, excitedly.

"Well, it's not mine. I'm just part of a crew, me and a bunch of other guys."

"How was it out there?" Frank asked Ryan.

"Yeah, Ryan, how was it? Kill a lot of bugs?" Dillon shifted on the bench and got onto his knees.

"Plenty. Nebraska got hit pretty hard by one of those mega asteroids. Must have busted up into a million pieces because the whole state was crawling with giant locusts."

"Wow, cool," Dillon said.

"No little brother," Ryan said, sternly, "it wasn't cool."

Dillon's expression changed and he looked like he was going to cry.

"He doesn't understand," Ally said, glaring at Ryan. She grabbed Dillon and started tickling him.

Sad or not, the boy couldn't help giggling.

"Sorry, Dillon. I wasn't being mean," Ryan apologized. "It's just that, well..."

"It's all right, Ryan," Wanda said and patted her son's hand. "We've all been through it."

"So are you still working in the triage?" Ryan asked Ally.

"No. I get to assist Dr. Tubbs. She's the head veterinarian in charge of livestock in the area."

"You mean Mom's actually letting you go there?" Ryan looked over at his mother. "Don't you think it's a little dangerous for her to be out in the field?"

"She'll be fine," Wanda assured Ryan. "They'll have patrols with them."

"You just be careful out there, Sis."

Ally gave her older brother a smile. "Quit your worrying, I'll be fine."

Wanda turned to Frank. "So, Jake tells me it was you that wrangled Ryan's transfer."

"Well, not entirely. I just helped things along."

"Then, who?" Ryan asked.

"My understanding is you'll be on special assignment."

"Doing what?"

"Driver for Celeste Starr."

"Are you serious?" Ryan was well acquainted with the woman and knew her from when the family vacationed almost a year ago in Africa. He'd found her attractive but quickly learned that she could be manipulative when she wanted to be.

"You don't sound too happy," Wanda said.

"I thought I was going to be doing something important."

"You are. You'll be ensuring her safety."

"Couldn't they get someone else?"

"She asked for you, personally," Frank said.

"She did?"

"You'll be shuttling her back and forth between Lick Observatory on Mount Hamilton and the Dish near the Stanford campus."

"So in other words, I'm just her chauffer."

"Basically, yes."

***

Ryan's unwillingness for the new assignment quickly turned to acceptance when he saw his vehicle. The black 2016 Mustang had a few scratches and the interior had seen some wear but Ryan didn't care: the 427 cubic inch engine under the hood made up for it.

As soon as he'd left Fort Mason, he navigated through the back streets and followed 19th Avenue until he hit the onramp onto Interstate 280.

There were derelict cars all along the side of the road, some even abandoned in the two right lanes.

Which meant an open straightaway in the fast lane.

Anxious to see what the car could do, Ryan pressed his boot down on the gas pedal. The beefy engine roared to life, throwing him back in his seat. Gripping the steering wheel tightly with both hands, he found the car to handle admirably. Racing down the freeway he was surprised to see the speedometer needle tick up to the 120-miles-per-hour mark. Maintaining his speed, he eased into the other lane. The wide tires hugged the road like cat claws dug into a carpet.

Satisfied with the test run, Ryan let up on the gas pedal and brought it down to a cruising speed of 60 miles an hour.

He glanced to his left and saw San Francisco International Airport down in the valley. There were maybe 10 commercial jets in the bay. Fuselages with wings sheered off, tailfins sticking out of the murky water. He could see planes that had crash-landed on the runways, the scorched airframes on the black tarmac.

He imagined most airports around the world looked the same.

The carnage hadn't been caused by bird strikes but by a new aviation threat.

Ryan spotted giant dragonflies darting back and forth in the sky over the airstrips and the nearby shoreline of the bay.

He returned his attention to the road as the highway came to a gradual bend. A ragged line of abandoned cars was next to the center divider. As he sped closer, he could see men searching through the vehicles, scavengers looking for food or water, anything of any value. A few of them turned when they heard the Mustang's mighty engine.

A man with a straggly beard, wearing a long trench coat stepped toward the edge of the fast lane and pointed his rifle.

Ryan goosed the gas pedal and swerved, clipping the gunman before he could even get off a shot. He checked the rearview mirror and saw the man he'd grazed, slowly getting up off the ground and shaking his fist.

"That'll teach you to get in my way," Ryan laughed. He continued barreling down the freeway bordered by groves of mushroom-shaped oak trees and rolling hills of wheat-colored grass.

Slowing down, he took the Page Mill Road off ramp and headed into the Stanford Hills. He followed a single lane road that had been converted into a paved hiking trail and stopped when he saw a military armor vehicle and four Eco-Marines standing guard outside a gated fence.

Ryan pulled up and put down his window. He looked at the approaching guard and told him who he was.

"We've been expecting you," the guard said. "Follow the trail all the way up."

Another guard opened the gate wide enough so Ryan could drive the Mustang through.

He followed the winding path for a hundred yards and slowed to a stop when he saw a family of three white-tailed deer grazing in a grove of eucalyptus trees. The six-point buck was big. Ryan figured it had to weigh upward of 200 pounds. The doe was slimmer. She was standing with her fawn, enjoying the sprouts around the tree trunks.

The buck raised its head suddenly and looked in Ryan's direction.

"Don't worry, I'm going." Ryan was about to accelerate when he heard the buck snort out a warning. The doe and fawn bolted into the brush.

Ryan gazed up into the trees.

A giant jumping spider leaped out of the branches, landed on the back of the stag, and sank its fangs deep into the deer's shoulder. The buck threw back its head. A horn tip poked into one of the spider's eyes, but the injury didn't deter the arachnid from continuing its attack.

It took only a few seconds for the paralyzing venom to take effect. The buck's legs gave out and it fell to the ground. Its eyes were glazed over as it lay on the ground, its side heaving. The spider methodically spun the deer into a cocoon so that it could drink its fluids at a later time.

Ryan looked up in the trees and saw more cocoons in the higher branches. He was repulsed by what he had just seen but knew there was nothing he could do about it and drove off.

A few minutes later he passed a sign warning hikers about the dangers of mountain lions.

Once he reached the hilltop, he saw the control station next to the 150-foot diameter communication satellite dish, and headed toward the building.

Ryan shut off the engine and climbed out of the Mustang. He saw half a dozen armed Eco-Marines guarding the perimeter. He could hear gas generators running in the rear of the building.

A young woman with red hair was standing outside the entrance. She was wearing a gray Stanford sweatshirt and jeans. "Welcome to the Dish, Ryan."

"Thanks."

"Come in and I'll introduce you to Milt."

Ryan followed Celeste inside the facility.

"So, what is it you're doing here?" he asked.

"We've been trying to contact a functioning satellite in hopes of recalibrating it and making it operational, but so far, we haven't had any luck." Celeste led the way down a hall and into a large room.

One entire wall was made up of electronic power supplies, tuners, amplitude modulators, oscillators, and various other pieces of equipment needed to broadcast and receive signals to and from space. Most of the instruments had black knobs and meters and reminded Ryan of an old stereo system his mother once had. The units were stacked on top of each other, housed in six-foot-tall metal cabinets.

There was an office area with some gray metal desks and chairs across the room that looked like it was no longer in use as they were piled with cardboard boxes.

A thin man with white hair was sitting in an old-style Naugahyde vinyl swivel chair in front of a long wood-grain console. He had on a pair of headphones and was adjusting a dial on a panel. He removed his headphones when he saw Ryan and Celeste enter.

"Ryan, this is Milt Tabors."

Milt slowly pulled himself out of the chair and stood to shake Ryan's outstretched hand.

"Good to meet you, sir," Ryan said giving the man a firm handshake but careful not to squeeze the old man's hand too much.

"Likewise, Ryan."

"Milt's been working here for..." Celeste paused and looked at Milt, "how long is it?"

"Since 1977. I was here when they launched Voyager 1 and 2."

"Really," Ryan said.

"Probably the only probes still working out there."

"You mean they're still operating after all these years?"

"I know, hard to believe," Milt said. "They're 12 billion miles out there in space and *still* transmitting signals back to Earth with a power source equivalent to a light bulb."

"That *is* amazing."

"It is when you consider we haven't been able to raise hide or hare from any of the Low Earth Orbit satellites and they're only 1,200 miles away."

"But don't we have astronauts up there?" Ryan asked.

"You mean the International Space Station?"

"Yeah."

"Haven't heard a peep out of them for months," Milt said.

"We keep trying," Celeste said, "but the spacecraft's been heavily damaged."

"How do you know?" Ryan asked.

"I've seen it from the observatory."

"So what, they're all dead?"

"We believe so, yes."

15

Wade and Debra stared at the bare shelves in the walk-in pantry. A half bag of canned goods was on the floor next to two plastic one-gallon milk jugs filled with the last of their drinking water.

"This is it, huh?" Wade said. "All of our reserves."

"You couldn't expect it to last forever."

"So what do we have, maybe a week?"

"I'd say we only have enough food and water for maybe three, four days."

"Then I'll have to go find some more."

"You're going to go out and ransack someone's house, break into a store?"

"If that's what it takes," Wade said.

"How does that make us any different from those lowlife thieves?"

"Deb, this is no time for a morality lesson." Wade turned and placed his hands on Debra's shoulders so he could look her straight in the eyes. "We've been barricaded in this house for five months. We have to face reality. Either I go out and find us some food and water, or we're all going to have to leave. Are you ready for that?"

"No, Wade."

"Besides, why should we go without when there's scum out there helping themselves to whatever they want?"

Amy screamed from the other room.

"What now?" Wade said. "Don't tell me it's another stupid spider."

"Wade, she's only a child."

"I know, but we have more important things to worry about right now." Wade hurried out of the kitchen and went into the living room. The first thing he noticed was that the sliding glass door that led out to the deck was wide open. He'd forgotten to lock it.

Three rough-looking men with guns were in his living room. He could see two more men out on the deck posted as lookouts, leaning against the railing, and holding rifles.

The man standing by the couch had a full black beard and a shaved head. He had hold of Amy. His dirty hand was covering her mouth. A pistol was tucked in his belt.

"Let go of my daughter," Wade said.

"You don't give the orders, I do," said the man sitting in Wade's favorite chair. He was wearing a filthy ball cap with the bill pointed backwards. The derelict's beard was gray and bushy. He had a crazy look in his eyes, especially when his fingers caressed the cold steel of the Colt revolver on the armrest.

The third man was thin and scraggily. His long dogface was lined with wrinkles like he'd spent most of his life homeless out in the sun. He looked at Wade and grinned while he urinated on the carpet in the corner of the room.

"Jesus, man, what the hell are you doing?" Wade said, disgustedly.

Debra stepped into the living room and huddled beside Wade. "My God, Wade. Who are these people?"

"Deb, get back in the kitchen."

"Hey, little lady, come join the festivities," said the man in the chair.

"You better do as he says." The dogface man didn't even bother to pull up his zipper as he turned and pointed his handgun.

Wade looked over at Amy and saw the fear in her eyes. He knew there was no point in trying to reason with them and he had to do something fast. The man in the chair must have seen the wheels turning in Wade's head.

"Take your gun out. Pinch the grip nice and slow." He grabbed the Colt off the armrest and pointed the gun at Wade.

Wade brought his hand up and used his forefinger and thumb to lift his Browning out of the shoulder holster.

"Now, throw it over on the couch."

Wade tossed the gun.

"Good. Now tell your old lady to come over here."

"Wade?" Debra clung tightly to his arm.

"What is it you want?" Wade said.

"I think it's perfectly clear what we want," the man in the chair said. He looked up at the man restraining Amy. "Take her into the bedroom."

"No!" Debra yelled. "Don't you dare!"

"Who's going to stop us? Certainly not him." The man in the chair grinned at Wade.

Amy kicked her legs when her abductor lifted her off the floor and started to carry her across the room.

"Take me instead!"

The man in the chair studied Debra.

"You heard me. I'll go." When the man didn't react, she said, "That is, unless you don't like..."

"Norton, lock the girl up," the man in the chair said. "Let's save her for later. We're going to have some fun out here."

Norton carried Amy down the hall. A few seconds later a door slammed and Norton returned.

"Get down on your knees, hands behind your head."

Wade dropped to his knees and clinched his fingers together behind his head.

"Now, you, get over here and take off your clothes."

"Deb, you don't have to do this," Wade said as his wife stepped further into the living room.

"I can't let them hurt Amy," Debra replied in a low voice.

"They're going to kill us either way."

Debra started to unbutton her shirt.

"Bastards, I'm going to kill you!" Wade yelled.

"Shut him up," the man in the chair said.

The dogface man strode over and pistol-whipped Wade across the face. He slumped forward on his hands and knees. Blood oozed out of the deep cut in his cheek and dripped onto the carpet.

Debra removed her shirt and dropped it on the floor. She made no attempt to undo her bra.

"Now the pants."

"Deb, no!" Wade's head was spinning but it didn't stop him from trying to get up.

A hammer cocked back and he froze.

He could hear Amy crying from her room. He'd never felt so helpless in his entire life. How could he save his family from these mad men?

Wade raised his head and looked out through the open sliding glass door.

One of the men outside was staggering back with a knife in his neck. The other man turned and a knife impaled his chest.

The three men in the living room were too busy watching Debra slipping down her pants to notice what was happening outside.

Wade saw a hand appear around the doorframe and pitch a throwing knife in his direction. As soon as it landed on the carpet, he picked it up and stabbed Dogface's right kneecap. The man howled and dropped his gun.

Norton went to pull his pistol out of his waistband.

Wade grabbed Dogface's gun and shot Norton in the forehead then put two bullets into Dogface's chest to shut him up.

The man in the chair trained his Colt on Wade.

Jack Stonewell stepped behind the Barcalounger and stuck the blade of a throwing knife deep into the sitting man's ear.

Wade got to his feet and rushed over to Debra, still wobbly having just stepped out of her jeans. "It's okay, I've got you," he said, catching her before she fell.

"Oh God, Wade. I thought for sure..."

"We're okay. Get dressed. Amy needs you."

Debra snatched her shirt and jeans from the floor, and rushed down the hall.

Jack went around the room, kicking each man on the floor with his steel-toed boot making sure the scumbags were dead.

"Not sure why I didn't get an invite to your party," Jack said, wiping the blood off the blade of his throwing knife on the shirt of the dead man in the recliner and slipping the dagger into a sheath on his belt along with half a dozen other knives.

"Glad you decided to crash it," Wade said. He went over to Jack and gave the man an appreciative hug.

"You know, this might be a good time to blow this pop stand. These guys are only the tip of the iceberg."

"What do you have in mind?"

"Tell Debra to pack up some clothes and get your stuff together. My truck's just outside."

"Where're we going?"

"Fort Mason."

16

Cass spent a couple hours studying Rob's technical manual so she could learn how to further program the robonaut so that it would respond to her voice and follow her commands. She was glad she had minored in mechanical engineering or she wouldn't have understood a word of it. The instructions were step-by-step with illustrations and helpful diagrams, and endless pages of complex electrical schematics.

Even with all that, she knew Rob's abilities were limited. Cass performed her first task and attached Rob's zero-g legs. Instead of booty feet, there were specially designed metal studs that could be inserted into sockets strategically positioned throughout the spacecraft both inside and outside so the robonaut would be anchored while moving about; and it made him look more human. Which Cass found comforting, and for some strange reason made her feel less alone.

She stood Rob next to the nadir window. The next thing she wanted to do was program the various voice commands she would be giving Rob and link them to the appropriate functions he would be performing. This took her longer than she expected, as she had to plug in different USB flash drives and download data to Rob's operating systems so its cameras and appendage parts functioned properly. There was also a microchip labeled to have artificial intelligence. Cass had no idea if it would be as advanced as iPhone's Siri. She was curious and decided to download the contents.

For a demonstration, Cass placed a joystick in front of Rob that was fastened on a plate with a three-foot-long post that she had screwed into the bulkhead.

She had a small microphone attached to her shirt collar so she could verbally communicate with Rob as well as a touch-screen tablet she could use to select various commands. She thought she would start with a simple introduction.

"Hello, Rob."

There was no response.

Cass looked at her tablet and saw that she hadn't activated the speech program. She rectified the problem and tried again.

"Hello, Rob."

"Hello," Rob replied in a computerized monotone.

"Do you know who I am?"

"Yes. You are Cass."

Of course, I am, you silly boy.

"That's right. I'm going to give you some commands."

"Very well," Rob said.

Was that compliance or did she just hear a tinge of eagerness in Rob's exchange.

"Grab the joystick."

Rob's right arm extended and its fingers curled around the black hub.

"Forward."

Rob pushed the joystick.

"Neutral."

The robonaut pulled the stick back to the center of the console.

"Backward," Cass said.

Rob brought the stick all the way back.

"Neutral."

Rob complied and pushed it midway.

"Left."

Again, the movement was correct. Just as it was when Rob was told to shift the stick in the opposite direction.

"Excellent," Cass said, pleased that the test had been a success.

"Thank you, Cass," Rob replied.

Cass was shocked, as she hadn't expected the robonaut to acknowledge being praised for his performance. Maybe she had been wrong underestimating Rob's potential.

For the next hour, Cass challenged Rob with a series of dexterity tests to see what the mechanical humanoid was capable of doing and what it couldn't do.

Rob passed with flying colors.

It was time to put Rob to work.

17

Jack pulled up to the guard shack and rolled down his window. An Eco-Marine approached while three others stepped around the truck, one standing by Wade's window while the other two guards inspected the cargo bed.

"We'd like to join up with your group," Jack said.

"Is that right?" the Eco-Marine said, eyeing Jack suspiciously. "Identification."

Jack and Wade took out their billfolds and handed over their driver licenses. Wade looked over his shoulder at Debra, sitting in the back seat of the crew cab with Amy. "Did you bring yours?"

"Yes, I have it right here." Debra unzipped a small duffle on the seat. She was about to reach inside when the guard ordered her to stop.

"Open your window and toss the bag out."

Debra let down the window. She held the bag out and dropped it on the cement.

One of the other guards walked around and picked up the duffle. He looked inside and said, "No weapons." He took out Debra's wallet, removed her driver license, and gave it to the guard in charge then handed the duffle back to Debra.

Debra leaned forward. "Please, we have nowhere else to go," she said, making sure the guard got a look at Amy sitting by her side.

"Park the truck over there and shut off your engine," the guard instructed.

Jack drove through the gate, parked in a stall where three other guards were waiting, and shut off the engine.

"Now what?" Wade asked Jack.

"Now we wait."

"I'm thirsty," Amy said.

"Here." Debra reached down and picked up the water jug on the floor mat. She removed the cap and tipped the plastic container so Amy could get a drink.

Wade glanced out the windshield at the rows of three-story buildings. He saw more than a hundred people out and about, most of them in civilian clothes. There were infantry fighting vehicles and armored personnel carriers in the parking lot along with modified heavy-duty commercial trucks with machineguns.

He could see a long building out on a pier. He looked through Jack's window and spotted the prison structures on Alcatraz Island out in the middle of the channel. "Think anyone's out there?"

"Probably. Don't tell me you want to go out there?"

"No. Not on your life."

"Someone's coming over," Debra said.

Wade watched as a man and a woman approached Jack's side of the truck. "They must be from the militia."

"Hi, there. I'm Wanda Rafferty-Travis and this is my husband, Frank."

Everyone in the truck returned the greeting while Wanda handed the driver licenses back.

"And you are?" Wanda asked the young girl sitting in the back seat.

"I'm Amy. I'm seven."

"Amy's almost eight," Debra said.

"You like school Amy?" Wanda asked.

"I guess so."

"You mean you have a real school here?" Debra asked.

"We have excellent teachers. My son, Dillon is a student. In fact, Amy will be in his class."

"Did you hear that, Amy?" Debra said. "You'll be making friends."

Amy smiled up at her mother.

"Let us show you where you'll be staying and then you can all unpack," Wanda said.

"Sounds good," Wade said. He opened his door and exited the truck. He opened the rear door and helped his wife and daughter out.

Jack got out and they all assembled in front of the truck.

"I'm afraid we only have accommodations in the barracks right now," Wanda said.

"That'll be fine," Wade said.

"Once you get settled in, I'll give you the grand tour," Frank said.

"So how do we earn our keep?" Jack asked.

"Have you any combat training?"

"You might say that."

"How about you, Wade?"

"I'm a lineman by trade, but I'm pretty handy with a gun."

"Not too bad with a knife either, if I do recall," Jack said, reminding Wade of what he had done back at his home.

Frank and Wanda couldn't help noticing all the knives strapped on Jack's belt.

"Jack was the American Knife Throwers Alliance champion two years in a row," Wade said.

"Impressive," Frank said. "Later, after I show you around, we can sit down and I'll explain what we do. Get you ready for a patrol."

"Sounds fair enough," Wade said. He put his arms around Debra and Amy. "See guys, everything is going to work out fine. We'll be safe here."

18

"Is it far?" Ally asked as they headed up a narrow country road into the hills.

"Another mile or so," Dr. Gemma Tubbs replied from behind the steering wheel of the van as they sped after their escort, tailgating so close that Ally was sure they were going to rear end the other vehicle.

Up ahead, two pickups were parked diagonally, blocking the road.

"Don't worry, they're ours," the veterinarian said, but didn't bother to slow down.

One of the trucks backed up and let them go through. Ally looked in her side mirror and saw the truck move back to reform the blockade.

A high fence ran along the roadside. Every so often, Ally would catch a quick glimpse of a sign. She could see numerous rows of solar panels high above on a grassy hill.

"So what are the solar panels for, Dr. Tubbs?"

"For the electric fence; or rather—the corral. It's the only way we can contain the herds so they don't wander off. Keeps out rustlers. You know, Ally, you can call me Gemma."

"Okay."

"We're here," Gemma said. She turned into a dirt turnaround and parked next to three RV motor homes in a horseshoe formation. There were also half a dozen four-wheel all-terrain bikes with cargo beds. "This is our home base and where we will be staying for the night."

Ally stepped out of the van and went around the back to help Gemma as she opened the rear doors to offload the medical supplies they had brought. "How many head of cattle did you say there were?"

"Rough count, maybe three hundred," Gemma said. "We also have about twenty horses, a good size flock of sheep, and a tribe of around two hundred goats."

"It's a shame we can't keep them at the fort," Amy said, lifting out a cardboard box and finding it surprisingly heavy.

"There's nowhere for them to graze down there. As you can see, there's plenty of grass to go around up here."

"So when do we get started?" Ally asked, adjusting her grip on the box.

"Right away. Go ahead and put that box in the back of that silver ATV. That's mine. Yours is the one next to it."

"You mean we're going up in those?"

"It's the only way to get medical supplies up there so we can tend to the animals."

"Dr. Tubbs, just say the word when you're ready." It was Max Simms. He'd been the one driving the escort vehicle. He was carrying an M16 assault rifle instead of his beloved grenade launcher.

Vince and Julie were slowly approaching. The Eco-Marines were carrying similar weapons, along with sidearms.

"No Ace and Johnny this time?" Gemma asked.

"They did a double rotation so I'm giving them some R&R."

"Aren't you the softy?"

"Don't let them hear that," Max said, nodding his head at his team. "Need any help with that?"

"Please. There's more vaccine and syringes in that box. You can leave the rest for later."

Max picked up the box and balanced it with one hand. He started over to the ATVs while Gemma closed up the van.

The five got on their bikes and started them up. Max led the way and they headed up a worn trail through the trees.

It took ten minutes to reach the gate. Max let his bike idle and climbed off. He went over to a control box, inserted a key, and opened the front panel. He flicked off a switch then locked the box.

He went over, unlocked the padlock, and swung the gate open. He got on his bike and followed everyone through the entrance. He closed the gate and fastened the padlock. Before he got back on the ATV, he opened another control box and reactivated the electrified gate.

Ally could see the grazing animals. She had never seen so many cattle, horses, sheep, and goats mingled together.

A roadway had been etched through the grass and led up to a massive steel beamed structure without walls. Rows of hay bales were stacked under the roof, twenty-feet up in the air. A forklift and a flatbed truck were parked nearby.

Everyone pulled up and turned off their bikes.

Ally was dismounting when she thought she saw something move between the hay bales. "Did anyone see that?"

"See what?" Max said.

"Over there," Ally said and pointed between two rows of hay.

"How big?"

"I'm not sure."

Max looked at Gemma. "What do you think?"

"There's alfalfa in there. Could be blister beetles."

"Shit, not those things again."

"Aren't they extremely toxic?" Ally asked.

"Very," Gemma said. "They excrete cantharidin, which is highly poisonous to the livestock."

"And can burn the flesh right off the bone," Vince said.

"Listen up Eco-Marines. Time to search and destroy." Max readied his M16 and started down one row. Vince and Julie aimed their weapons and chose separate rows.

"We better get back in case they flush one our way," Gemma warned. They moved away but still had a view of the Eco-Marines.

"I see it!" Julie hollered. She fired off a steady barrage, ripping apart a hay bale and sending straw flying everywhere.

Ally was horrified when a giant blister beetle raced down a row, heading directly at her and Gemma. Vince was chasing the beetle but he couldn't get a clear shot without striking either Ally or Gemma.

The six-foot long beetle came to a sudden halt, raised its anus, and blasted Vince who ran directly into the hot chemical stream. Vince dropped his rifle and grabbed his face, screaming. Amy could actually see the flesh bubbling on his face. Still screaming, he fell to his knees.

Max came around just as the beetle was about to flee and riddled the carapace with holes, emptying his clip. "Son of a bitch!"

"There's another one," Julie yelled and began firing.

Ally and Gemma ran over to Vince. He was in a great deal of pain, curled up on his side. He'd stopped screaming but was lying there, whimpering.

Julie came running up. "I nailed it." She took one look at Vince. His face looked hideous, like a burn victim that had been trapped in a three-alarm fire. "Oh, jeez."

Gemma assessed his injury. She looked up at Max who was standing over her. "He needs to go to triage. I don't think there's anything I can do for him."

"Vince? Can you hear me?" Max shouted.

"Oh God. I can't see," Vince cried out.

"Take it easy, son," Max said. "We're taking you back. Just hold on."

"I really must stay here," Gemma said.

"We can't leave you alone."

"I'll stay," Ally said.

"No, you don't get it. You're not safe out here without our protection."

"I can take Vince," Julie said.

"You sure?"

"Max, I'm an Eco-Marine."

"All right. Let's all go back to the motor homes. Then we can load Vince in the transport and Julie can take him back." Max looked at Gemma. "I'll stay."

"Okay," Gemma said.

They got Vince to his feet, helped him over to Julie's ATV, and laid him on his back on the short cargo bed with his legs dangling off the back.

"Let's head out!" Max yelled.

The four bikes roared off down the dirt road.

19

Cass rolled out of the Quest airlock and clipped on her tether. Her Extravehicular Mobility Unit space suit was bulky and weighed 280 pounds on Earth, but out in space the only strain on her body was that it was restricting and cumbersome.

Several inner pressurized layers of insulation protected her body; the outer skin of the suit both bulletproof and fire-resistant. Without the pressurized suit, Cass would become unconscious within 15 seconds, and her body would swell to twice its size—and she would die a relatively excruciating death.

Her cap was equipped with a microphone and earphones.

"Rob, exit the airlock."

Cass gazed through the clear impact-resistant plastic of her helmet and watched Rob float out. She grabbed its tether and secured the anchor end to the spacecraft to prevent the robonaut from drifting haplessly out into space. She had taken extra precautions and had covered the humanoid's body with material she had fashioned out of thermal sheets to prevent the extreme temperatures from damaging Rob's operating systems and mechanisms.

Her first undertaking was to try and repair at least one of the four ARISS antennas that were used for transmitting signals on amatuer radio frequencies from the space station down to Earth. The second task was to dislodge the chunk of asteroid blocking the hatchway into the Soyuz escape module. None of which would be easy, especially as this was only Cass's second spacewalk.

She was shocked to see the extensive structural damage to the trusses, which were the backbones of the space station connecting the various modules, the solar panels, and the radiators used to dispel heat.

Cass grabbed Rob by the arm as the robonaut didn't have self-propulsion and activated the thruster attached to her life-support system backpack. She gave it a short burst propelling them between the cylindrical superstructures until they reached the module that housed the antennas.

"Rob, stay." The robonaut responded by latching its zero-g legs to the module's outer shell.

She did a complete circumnavigation and found only one antenna. The asteroids had scraped off the other three. She assessed the damage. The antenna mast was bent but hadn't snapped apart and the ground plate had lifted up. She figured the cable had disconnected from the coupler and was the reason why she was unable to receive or broadcast a signal.

"Rob, come," Cass ordered. She waited for Rob to disengage then pulled its tether. The robonaut sailed over the twenty-foot span. She put out her gloved hand and stopped Rob before it could collide into her.

"Rob, stay."

Rob attached its foot studs in the sockets next to the base of the antenna.

"Well done," Cass said.

"Thank you, Cass."

She still wasn't used to Rob addressing her back, especially when she was issuing it basic commands as though it were a dog.

Cass opened the tool belt mounted on her suit's chest. She had to look at a mirror attached to her right wrist in order to see the set of magnetic tools. She chose an adjustable wrench and took out a clear pouch.

"Rob, hold tool." She handed the wrench to the robonaut.

The job was simple enough; remove the antenna mast, some nuts, and washers and fix the problem under the ground plate. In a gravity environment and with bare hands, the task would be routine. But in space with zero gravity, it was going to be a definite chore.

Cass decided it would be better to direct Rob and have the robonaut disassemble the mast so she could gather the parts and put them in the pouch for when it came time to reassemble the antenna. The last thing she wanted was for an intricate piece to get away from her and drift out into space.

Guiding Rob's hand, Cass adjusted the wrench and set the teeth around the nut holding the tip of the antenna in place.

"Rob, counter clockwise turn."

The robonaut twisted the wrench a full turn.

"Repeat."

Again, its hand turned the tool. Cass kept repeating the command until the nut came completely loose. She grabbed the mast and secured it to a brace on the truss with an anchor strap. The nut slowly came off, as did the antenna bezel and two washers. She swiped at the pieces with her thick glove, catching the bezel and washers but not the nut, which was critical in putting everything back together. She couldn't open her glove or she would release the other parts. She frantically tried stuffing them in the pouch.

"No, no, come on. Get in there!" She glanced up and saw the nut drifting...

Rob's fingers closed around the nut.

"Oh, my God. You caught it without me telling you."

Rob extended its hand.

"Thank you, Rob," Cass said and took the nut and placed it in the pouch.

"You are welcome, Cass."

This was incredible. Rob had just exhibited the capability to problem solve—and without having to be told.

They continued to work on the antenna. It was just as she suspected, the cable under the ground plate had become disconnected. Rob methodically reconnected the cable, fastened down the ground plate, and reassembled the antenna mast and completed the job in a matter of minutes, which should have taken an astronaut considerably more time.

"Good job, Rob."

"Thank you, Cass."

"You're welcome."

Something flashed past Cass's visor. She watched it crash through a single solar panel like a rock hurling through a pane glass window. She turned her head and saw a field of asteroids coming her way. Some were the size of softballs, others as big as a house.

"Rob, hold on!" she yelled. Even though she couldn't hear them whizzing by, she could see the damage the asteroids were doing to the space station. Her worst fear was getting struck. It would only take a grape-size rock to rip through her spacesuit even though it was constructed to stop a bullet. This was certainly no time to put it to the test.

Cass saw a large chunk coming at her and pushed away.

A sharp edge of the rock cut through her tether.

She felt herself float away from the truss and slowly begin to tumble, helmet over boots. After the third spiral, she was disoriented. Her breathing was erratic and sounded extremely loud like she had overexerted herself from a strenuous run. She thought of using her thrusters but was afraid of propelling herself in the wrong direction.

Cass knew split-second thinking was critical in her situation and there was no time for indecision, but she didn't know what to do so she continued to drift farther and farther away...

20

"I guess this is home sweet home," Wade said. A single overhead light bulb in the middle of the ceiling illuminated their assigned room. It was sparsely furnished with a single Army surplus cot for Wade and twin bunk beds for Debra and Amy. There were three metal lockers to stow their clothes and belongings. A rickety-looking chair and an old wooden desk with a drawer missing were butted up against a wall.

"Wade? Amy wants a kiss goodnight," Debra said.

He walked across the room to the top bunk. Debra made sure Amy was snug and warm and adjusted the top of the heavy military blanket under Amy's chin.

"I know it isn't what you're used to," Wade said, "but I think you're going to like it here. You'll get to go to school and play with other kids. That should be fun, right?"

"Do I have to go to school?"

"I'm afraid so."

"Okay."

"Sleep tight...and what do we say?" Wade said.

"Don't let the bedbugs bite," they said together as it was their nightly ritual. Wade kissed his daughter on the forehead.

"Goodnight, honey," Debra said and gave Amy a kiss. She reached up and flicked off the wall switch, casting the room into darkness.

Wade and Debra ambled across the room. They looked out the third-story window and could see slivers of the Golden Gate Bridge and Alcatraz Island in the night fog.

"Quite the view," Wade said.

Debra slipped her arm in the crook of Wade's arm.

He leaned down and kissed her.

"I wouldn't be getting any ideas," Debra said. "Not with our daughter in the room."

"Don't worry," Wade said. "I doubt very seriously if that cot could hold the two of us, let alone me."

"How long do you think we'll stay here?"

"I really don't know. But at least we'll be safer here than out there."

"Thank God, Jack came around when he did," Debra said. "I don't know what I would have..." the words were replaced with tears.

"It's all right. Try not to think about it," Wade said and put his arm around her.

There was a faint knock at the door.

Wade stepped away from Debra. He went over, opened the door a crack, and peeked out.

"You guys settling in?" Jack asked from out in the hall.

Wade opened the door wider. "Yeah, how about yourself?"

"Never thought I'd be bunking in a barracks again. Thought I'd hit the showers."

"Let me grab my kit. I want to brush my teeth before turning in." Wade went over to his locker and grabbed his toiletry bag. "I won't be long," he said to Debra and closed the door behind him.

"How's Debra holding up?" Jack asked as they headed down the hall.

"She's still a little shaken up."

"Yeah, that was pretty rough."

Wade turned to his friend. "Yeah, well it would have turned out a lot worse if you hadn't shown up when you did."

"Glad to have been of service," Jack said with a smile. He had a towel slung over his shoulder. He was barefoot but was still wearing his shirt and jeans.

Wade noticed he hadn't taken off his belt of throwing knives. "Expecting trouble?"

"Never let your guard down," Jack said. "No matter what."

"Even on the crapper?"

"Especially on the crapper," Jack grinned and the two of them laughed.

"Jesus Christ!" a man yelled from around the corner.

"Oh my God!" a woman screamed. "Get if off of me!"

"Damn things are everywhere!"

Wade and Jack ran around to the main room which had two rows of twin bunks stretched the length of the barracks, enough to sleep over 120 people. Just about everyone was on their feet, many moving away from the beds. Most of the overhead lights were off, controlled at a box at the far end of the room. Even though the beds had been vacated, there was still movement on the mattresses. Wade saw something in the gloom that looked like a large lobster without claws, crawling across a blanket.

Then he caught a glimpse of another one on a nearby bunk. Hell, they were everywhere.

"Sucker bit the shit out of me," a man yelled.

"Damn, I'm being eating alive," another man hollered.

Someone started firing a gun.

"Put that away idiot before you shoot someone!" yelled a large man. He came over and grabbed the pistol from the frightened trigger-happy shooter. "Everyone, listen up! Take out your knives, anything you can kill them with, but no guns!"

A lot of the people were wearing only their underwear and were fighting the things off with their hands, stomping them with their feet or hitting them with their rifle stocks or anything sharp.

A man wearing only a T-shirt and boxers backed toward Wade and Jack.

"What the hell is going on?" Wade asked the man.

"Some fool must have brought in some life forms."

"Life forms?" Wade asked.

"Yeah, those alien things the bugs eat."

The man saw the questioning look on Wade's face.

"You didn't know?"

"I've seen plenty of giant bugs but I never knew what caused them."

The man backed up as four lobster-sized bugs skittered across the floor.

"Watch this," Jack said. He pulled four knives out of their sheaths and held two in each hand. He cocked back both arms then flung a single knife from each hand. Each blade hit the mark and impaled a bug to the hardwood floor. He drew back his arms again and threw the two remaining knives, pegging the other two bugs to the floor.

"Wow, that was pretty fancy," the man said, genuinely impressed.

The inside of the barracks sounded like a major barroom brawl as everyone scrambled to kill the infestation. Wade thought he'd heard every curse word in the book until tonight.

"Look! It's happening," the man in his skivvies said, pointing at a specific bottom bunk then backing away.

Wade and Jack approached the bed, slowly. The top sheet was rumpled and the blanket was on the floor. It looked like the occupant had suddenly scrambled out of the bed in a big hurry. There was something moving under the sheet, bulging the thin fabric—getting bigger as they watched as though it was being gradually inflated.

The big man that had ordered everyone not to use their guns, strode over and stood next to Wade. He stared at the strange phenomena. "You guys are in for a treat. It's not very often you get to witness an actual transformation." He stepped over and eased the sheet off, then shined a flashlight on the bed.

"Holy crap!" Wade said, unable to contain his surprise.

The six-legged bug on the mattress had a light-brown, flat oval-shaped hard-shelled body. At first glance, it was the size of a man's hand but as Wade watched—it was impossible not to—it steadily grew and grew. It was unbelievable; truly mesmerizing and was happening so fast. The bug was almost the size of a roasting pan.

"It would be a good idea to kill it about now," the big man said. "A blade behind the head works the best."

Jack took one of his flat knives and stabbed the bug, almost severing its head.

"That was really incredible to witness," Wade said.

"Yeah. By the way, I'm Crandall Green. I'm in charge of this floor."

"Good to meet you," Wade said and shook Crandall's hand. Jack introduced himself and the two men shook hands.

"Do you have family here?" Wade asked.

"Just my wife, Shelly. She teaches school here."

"What grade?"

"First through fourth."

"My daughter's seven," Wade said. "She'd be in first grade."

"Looks like she'll be in Shelly's class."

"So has this happened before?" Jack asked.

"Oh, you mean the infestation? Yeah, I'm afraid so. Usually after the Eco-Marines eradicate an impact site."

Wade gave Crandall a questioning look.

"From the meteorites. As the life forms are so small, they're difficult to see. They cling to everything. Clothes, boots, even get in your hair if you aren't careful."

"Are they harmful to humans?" Wade asked.

"Not that we know of. For some unexplainable reason, they're only able to morph insects."

"Well, we should be grateful for that," Jack said.

"Yeah," Crandall said. "One sec... Hey everyone!" he shouted to the people in the large room. "Anyone that's been bit, get over to the infirmary on the double!"

A woman with a blanket draped around her shoulders, strolled over and joined them.

"This is my wife, Shelly," Crandall said and introduced Wade and Jack.

"Nice to meet you," Wade said. "Your husband says you teach school here."

"That's right," Shelly replied.

"Then you'll be teaching my daughter."

"What's her name?"

"Amy."

"I look forward to meeting her."

"Well, I think I better get back to my family," Wade said.

Wade and Jack returned to the hallway and walked to the restroom. It was a large public room with ten sinks in front of a mirrored wall and an equal amount of stalls with toilets. A tiled entry led to the showers. Wade washed up at a sink and brushed his teeth while Jack went to take a quick shower.

"See you in the morning," Wade yelled out as he slipped out the door. Jack said something but it was difficult to hear his reply over the running water. Wade had a laugh visualizing Jack standing under the shower, naked, but still wearing his knife belt.

When Wade got back to the room, Debra was standing next to the bunk with a concerned look on her face. "All I could hear was people yelling and screaming. Thank God, Amy didn't wake up. What in the world was going on out there?"

"Bedbugs."

21

Cass felt a tug on her gloved hand, which stopped her from somersaulting through space. She glanced sideways inside her helmet and saw that it was Rob that had grabbed her by the hand.

She couldn't believe it. The robonaut had actually come to her rescue. It pulled on its tether, creating momentum, and propelled them back onto a truss ledge.

"Oh my God, Rob. Thank you, thank you so much."

"You are welcome, Cass."

Her lips were parched so she took a drink from the straw-end of her drink bag. It took a minute for her breathing to resume to a steadier rate. The ordeal of almost being stranded out in space had taken a heavy toll on her nerves. She decided repairing the antenna was enough for now and would leave the task of trying to remove the asteroid blocking the access passage to the Soyuz for the next spacewalk.

They glided back through the superstructures and entered the space station airlock. If it weren't for Rob's assistance, Cass would never have been able to put on the bulky spacesuit on her own. She had programmed a step-by-step procedure into Rob's operation system along with a reverse process so that Rob could assist her in removing her spacesuit. She stepped into the frame that supported the upper half of the suit and her life-support backpack.

Cass was relieved when Rob removed her helmet by sliding the release tabs and twisting the cover. Even though the air in the compartment was stale and not at all refreshing, it was better than being cooped up inside the helmet. Rob turned each one of her gloves enough so they detached from the sleeves. She raised her arms and slid out of the upper portion of her suit and onto the deck, grabbing onto handholds so that she didn't float awkwardly. Rob was anchored and held the boots of her suit so she could pull her legs out of the lower portion of the suit.

She removed her skintight ventilation undergarment that fit around her body like spandex and was surprised she hadn't panicked and soiled her diaper almost being lost in space; the absorbent material intended for extended spacewalks without potty breaks.

It felt liberating, floating naked, but also strangely erotic knowing Rob was recording her every moment with its cameras.

She slipped a sweatshirt over her head then put on a pair of shorts and woolen socks.

"Well, what do you say we go see if the radio works?"

"I don't understand the command," Rob said in a monotone voice.

"Let's go see if the radio works."

"The radio in the Columbus."

"Yes, Rob. How did you know where it was?"

"All equipment and their locations are in my data bank."

"So they are. Silly me," Cass said and smiled.

"Who is Silly Me?"

"Just an expression." Cass didn't want to confuse Rob, if that was even possible.

He was proving to be truly amazing. Did she just say he*? Was she that desperate for human contact that she was actually considering Rob as a fellow astronaut instead of just a machine? Whatever gets you through the day.*

"Rob. Follow me," Cass said. She propelled out of the changing chamber and turned at the first junction into the Destiny module and then into the Harmony module. Rob stayed right on her heels. She performed an elegant acrobatic move like a synchronized swimmer under water and glided into the laboratory module, Columbus.

Plexiglas enclosures on flat surfaces occupied one curved wall containing various test subjects. White lab rats and guinea pigs were loosely strapped down, study subjects on the effects of weightlessness. Only a handful were still alive.

Cass looked into a glass box and saw over 200 fruit flies clinging to a fabric wall and another 100 lying dead in a big heap after their immune systems had failed due to microgravity. A colony of ants in the next habitat seemed to be fairing better as they were still actively scampering about in their pressurized ant farm. She moved to the next display case that had minute air holes and saw an intricate web configuration and its maker in the center—a gold-colored spider with long spindly legs and a body the size of a dime.

She drifted over to the amateur radio and switched it on. Loud static came out of the speaker, so she turned down the volume.

"Rob. Anchor beside me."

The robonaut planted its stud feet into the bulkhead, an arm's-length away from Cass.

She adjusted the dial to a designated frequency band and began a voice check to see if she could get a response.

"This is NA1SS. Is there anyone out there that can hear me?" Her throat felt raspy so she grabbed a thin water pouch that she'd brought along and squirted a small amount of water out of the tube into her mouth. A few tiny goblets escaped out of the end of the spout and drifted away.

Cass waited attentively for a reply and heard nothing but white noise.

She switched to the next frequency.

Again, she repeated the call sign of the International Space Station used by American astronauts and got nothing.

Even though she wasn't getting a reply, it didn't mean there wasn't a ham radio operator down on Earth that might eventually hear her. They could be on the other side of the planet for all she knew. Or maybe they had turned off their radios to conserve power. Or maybe she and Rob hadn't fixed the antenna properly.

Or maybe everyone was dead down there and it was all a big waste of time.

She wasn't ready to give up hope.

Not yet.

She was about to try another frequency when she noticed something on Rob's visor. She turned her body so she could lean in and take a closer look.

Thin, whitish shapes detached from the convex shield and floated in front of Cass's face.

The back of her head started to itch. Something was crawling in her hair. She reached up, combed her fingers through her thick curls then looked down at her hand...

And watched in horror as tiny alien life forms wriggled on her palm.

22

"The drive up to the observatory is rather treacherous," Celeste said, clutching her seatbelt harness cinched tight across her chest. She held onto the handgrip above her side window as they came up on another curve.

"What happened to your last driver?" Ryan asked.

"Said he didn't like heights. Gave him vertigo."

Ryan had to admit the drive up Quimby Road and over the first mountain had been a hazardous trek with its narrow roads and hairpin curves, each bend so tight that he was forced to slow down to the posted speed limit of ten miles an hour. It was a tedious drive; one that Ryan didn't relish having to repeat too often.

He gunned the powerful engine halfway into the turn as they headed up a short straightaway only to have to slow down as they came upon the next curve, which was frustrating. Still he took the opportunity to rev the muscle car with a quick burst then eased on the brake, releasing some pent-up tension. "How far is it from the Dish to the observatory?"

"Twenty-five miles. You know this isn't a race."

"You're the one that wanted me as your driver." Ryan downshifted into a lower gear as they headed down a steep stretch of road that took them to a T-junction where he turned right onto Mt. Hamilton Road. He was able to speed up a bit as the roadway was a little wider with fewer turns but it wasn't long before he had to slow down as they were back to traversing up the mountain.

He shot a quick glance over at Celeste and saw her peek over her shoulder before snapping her head around to look out the windshield.

"What's with the arsenal in the backseat?" she asked, referring to the two M16 assault rifles, the open duffle containing three fully loaded handguns with additional full clips, and 20 boxes of ammunition.

"It's in case we come across any banditos," Ryan said.

"This isn't Mexico."

"Okay, highwaymen."

"Now you sound like Robin Hood."

"I think you get the idea."

For the next fifteen minutes they continued up the winding road, each nerve-wracking curve giving them incredible panoramic views of the haze-shrouded valley below and the undulating mountain ranges stretching as far as the eye could see.

There were no guardrails to prevent them from driving off the side of the road and plummeting down the sheer precipice. Even though there was no opposing traffic on the extremely narrow two-way road, Ryan had to be on the lookout for rockslides and sections where the blacktop was pitched higher than the ground, creating a groove. One wrong turn and one of the mustang's front tires could slip off the pavement and cause Ryan to lose control of the car—and down they would go.

Ryan clutched the steering wheel with both hands, sat forward a bit, and pulled the back of his sweat-covered shirt away from the leather seat. "Why'd they have to put so many turns in this road?"

"Lick Observatory was built in 1876 and the only way to get building material up the mountain was by mules and horse-drawn wagons, which meant the road couldn't be very steep."

"Makes sense." Ryan checked his speed as they came to another hairpin bend. He gazed out at the sprawling vista for a split second but quickly returned his attention back to his driving or he would have driven off the road for sure. Now he knew exactly what the other driver meant when he said he had experienced vertigo. "How high is this place?"

"Just over four thousand feet."

"Do all observatories have to be on the top of a mountain?"

"It helps if you want to avoid light pollution."

"You mean air pollution?" Ryan said.

"No. In order for these telescopes to work properly there can't be cloud cover or any obscuring ambient light. The city was so supportive it even agreed to replace all their streetlamps with low pressure sodium lights, which further reduced the light pollution."

"Well, I'm guessing none of that's a problem, as most of the city has gone dark."

"Sadly, yes. We're almost there, but do you mind pulling over?"

"Why?"

"Would you rather I puked in your car?"

Ryan hit the brakes and stopped in the middle of the road.

Celeste flung open her door. She leaned out and hurled up her toast and coffee they'd had for breakfast at the Dish before getting on the road.

"You okay?" Ryan asked.

"Yeah," Celeste said and spat on the ground. She wiped her mouth with her shirtsleeve and sat back in the car.

They arrived at the Lick Observatory a few minutes later. Ryan turned right and followed the steep roadway that took them to the front entrance of the main building with a white dome on either end. He parked the car and climbed out of the Mustang. He took a moment to stretch and work out the kinks. He hadn't realized how tense his shoulder and neck muscles had become due to the terrifying drive up.

Celeste walked over to a sparse railing with only two strands of thick wire as a barrier protecting anyone from falling over the edge to a sure death. She gazed out over the terrain. "You can actually see the Bay Area from here."

Ryan joined her and took in the view. It was breathtaking, like being on top of the world, and to think they were just four thousand feet above sea level. He couldn't even imagine what it must look like standing on the peak of Mt. Everest.

There were old houses scattered about the observatory site where researchers lived and slept during the day as the astronomers worked at night. Some of the buildings had been built over a century ago.

"What do you think?' Celeste said, commenting on the magnificent view. "Was it worth the drive?"

"I'll say."

"Let's go inside."

"Go ahead. I'll be right in," Ryan said. He went back to the car while Celeste started walking toward the front steps of the building. He pulled out his sidearm and checked the magazine then opened the car door and grabbed an assault rifle from the back seat.

He ran up the steps, opened the door, and stepped into a high-ceiling alcove where there were two tall doors across from each other, an entrance to a hallway, and a large black bust of James Lick on a pedestal.

"Take a look around if you want," Celeste said and turned right at the hall to go talk with her colleagues, who like herself, were members of the Astronomical Consortium tasked with pinpointing the locations of every meteorite impact site.

Ryan read the brief biography on a plaque that said James Lick was from Pennsylvania. Ryan wondered if he was Amish because he had a full beard with a clean upper lip or was that just the style for men back in those days. He thought it was strange that a man who made pianos for a living and didn't have a scientific background would fund the money to build an astronomical observatory on the top of a mountain peak.

He went into the hall that branched off to his left and right. Photographs of the various observation domes were displayed on the walls along with blank, flat screens.

After a while, he decided to go outside where there were wrought iron tables and chairs. He sat down to enjoy the morning sun and before he knew it, he'd dozed off.

"Hey, Ryan. Wake up!"

Ryan opened his eyes as Celeste gave him a stern shake. "What, don't tell me you're ready to go back already?"

Celeste sat in the chair next to him. "Not just yet."

He noticed she had a notebook in her hand. "What do you have there?"

"New coordinates for the latest impact sites."

"So, what's up?"

"Have you ever heard of the Phaeton Hypothesis?"

"No. What's that?"

"There's a theory that a fifth planet once orbited between Mars and Jupiter."

"Seriously?"

"It was even given a name. Phaeton, from Greek mythology."

"Never heard of it. What makes anyone think there was another planet?"

"When it was discovered there was an inconsistency in the distances of the planets in our solar system from the sun."

"What kind of inconsistencies?" Ryan asked.

"Mercury is 35 million miles from the sun," Celeste began. "Then there's Venus, which is 67 million miles away and twice the distance. Earth is 93 million and Mars is 142 million. But when you look at the distance from the sun to Jupiter, it suddenly jumps to 484 million suggesting that there's a planet missing."

"So what happened to it?"

"Well, instead of an actual planet, there's an asteroid belt between Mars and Jupiter. Some scientists believe it used to be the hypothetical planet, Phaeton, and due to some cosmic event the planet was destroyed and became the asteroid belt."

"So why are you telling me this?"

"My colleagues and I strongly believe some of those asteroids managed to break away from their normal orbital path and are now circling our planet."

"You mean the meteorites?"

"Exactly. And that's not all. You know how scientists are always trying to prove there's life on Mars?"

"Yeah."

"Well, there's one thing we now know for certain."

"What's that?"

"There was definitely life on the planet, Phaeton."

"Which would explain the alien life forms."

"You got it, but there's a bigger problem."

"Bigger than giant bugs taking over the world?"

"Remember that comet that supposedly killed all the dinosaurs 65 million years ago and sent the planet into an ice age?"

"Yeah."

"It was estimated to be 6 miles across and created a 100-mile wide crater when it struck."

"Don't tell me there're asteroids up there that big?"

"We're calling it: Mother Lode. And its girth is close to 12 miles wide."

"That's twice the size and you think it's going to strike?"

"It's only a matter of time before Mother Lode reaches orbital decay."

A young man ran out of the building and came over to Ryan and Celeste.

"You have a phone call on the landline," he told Celeste. "It's Mr. Tabors."

"Thanks." Celeste got up from the bench. Ryan followed her inside and they went down the hall into a room that used to be the gift shop. The receiver of an old-style rotary phone was lying on a countertop. Celeste picked it up. "Hi, Milt." She listened for a moment.

Ryan saw a surprised look come over her face as her eyes opened wide.

"Oh my God," she said. "That's fantastic news." She placed the receiver back on the cradle.

"What is it?" Ryan asked.

"Milt picked up a transmission from the International Space Station."

"But I thought you said they were all dead?"

"I was wrong!" Celeste yelled. She jumped up and down like an excited child about to unwrap a very special Christmas present. She was so overjoyed she gave Ryan a big kiss.

When their lips parted, he couldn't help but grin. "Maybe you should be wrong more often."

23

By midmorning, Ally estimated that she and Gemma had inoculated over fifty livestock. The cattle had been the easiest as they were generally too preoccupied grazing and weren't bothered by a tiny needle. The sheep and goats were less receptive than the bovine and it was sometimes necessary to restrain them. Ally had to pin the noncomplying animal to the ground while Gemma administered the vaccines that were intended to strengthen their immune systems and keep them healthy.

Max stood close by and kept watch with his M16 cradled across the crook of his arm. He turned around and gazed up at the hillcrest. "We've got company."

Ally glanced up. She raised her hand to her brow and shaded her eyes against the bright sun. She could see the silhouette of a giant insect a hundred yards away, crawling over the low grass. That's when she heard the sound of approaching engines on the other side of the rise.

Ally and Gemma looked at Max.

"Be ready to run," he said.

Three ATV's came over the crest and stopped short of hitting the giant insect, which formed itself into a huge ball and began rolling down the hillside.

"Run!" Max yelled.

Ally grabbed the satchel with the medical supplies off the ground and dashed across the field alongside Gemma and Max. She looked over her shoulder at the massive sphere spinning after them. It reminded her of the scene in the Indiana Jones movie when Harrison Ford was trying to escape from being mowed down by the boulder in the cave.

"It's no use, we can't outrun it," Max said and veered off to the left like a split end avoiding a tackle. Ally and Gemma stayed right on his heels.

The massive gray ball spun past them and continued down the incline, scattering the animals along the way until it reached a grove of oak trees and disappeared from sight.

"What was that?" Ally asked as they came to a halt to catch their breath.

"Armadillidiidae," Gemma replied.

"A what?"

"One hell'uva big roly poly," Max laughed then glanced back up the hill.

The three ATV's came down the ridge and parked twenty feet away. The riders climbed off and grabbed their guns.

"When did you get back?" Max asked.

"About half an hour ago," Julie replied.

"We figured we were rested enough." Ace gave Max a friendly wave. Johnny greeted everyone with a nod.

"How's Vince doing?"

"Second degree burns," Julie said.

"Can he see?"

"The doctors said he'll have his sight back in a few days."

"Damn blister bugs."

"You want us to set up a perimeter?" Johnny asked.

"Yes." Max looked at Gemma. "How many more do you plan on doing today?"

"How many syringes do we have left?" Gemma asked Ally.

Ally opened the satchel and did a quick inventory. "Thirteen large doses and seventeen for the smaller animals."

"I'd say we have about three, maybe four hours of work left to do."

"We'll set up a four-point perimeter around the two of you," Max said. "That way we'll be able to warn you of any danger."

The pastureland was relatively flat with a few undulating slopes. Every so often Max would raise his arm and signal to his team when they came upon an entry hole leading down into a large burrow big enough to drive a small car down inside. He would yell out, "Fire in the hole!" as one of the Eco-Marines tossed in a fragmentation grenade, that once it exploded, collapsed the tunnel, and buried any monstrous creature lurking down under.

They came across a few cows that had decided to get out of the sun and were lying partially on their stomachs in the grass under some overhanging branches.

Ally and Gemma walked over slowly not wanting to disturb the small herd.

"That cow over by that tree looks like it just gave birth recently," Gemma said, pointing to the black and white bovine with the saggy underbelly.

"Where's the calf?" Ally asked.

"Good question. Let's go check in those trees. Maybe it just wandered off."

Gemma looked over her shoulder and signaled to Johnny who was not too far away. "We need to search for a missing calf."

Johnny quickly jogged over. "Let me lead the way."

The Eco-Marine readied his M16 and started through the trees. Ally and Gemma followed close behind. They hadn't gone more than fifty feet when they came across a gross sight.

"Jesus, what is that thing?" Johnny said, and aimed his assault rifle at the hideous white creature latched onto the side of the small calf down on the ground. It was as big as a tabby cat with a translucent body and was sucking the blood from its host.

Ally could actually see the crimson blood filling up its gullet as though it were gasoline being pumped into a tank.

"It's an assassin bug nymph," Gemma said.

"Wait a minute, I thought morphed bugs couldn't procreate?" Johnny said.

"Did you really just say *procreate*?" Julie said, joining the group.

"Uh, yeah."

"To answer your question, they can't," Gemma said. "This little bugger must have eaten an elf."

"What did you call it? An elf?" Ally asked.

"Just my little nickname for extraterrestrial life form instead of alien life forms. Can you pull it off?"

Even though Ally was wearing a pair of nitrite gloves the slimy nymph still felt creepy when she grabbed it around the head and pulled back until the proboscis was completely out of the docile calf. She placed the bloodsucker on the ground. Johnny played executioner and crushed it with a large rock.

"Is the calf okay?" Ally asked.

"It's suffering temporary paralysis from the nymph's venom. Let's give it a few minutes and then see if we can get it on its feet."

"You guys better hurry up in there," Max shouted. He was standing on the outskirts of the trees. Ace was by his side with his back turned, gazing out at the pastureland.

"Why, anything wrong?" Gemma called back.

"You might say that," Max replied.

Ally could hear the cows vocalizing their alarm like an agitated herd before a stampede. "Is something attacking the livestock?"

"We better go see," Gemma said. "The calf should be fine here."

They hurried through the trees and reached the spot where the small group of cows had been languishing in the shade but the animals had already gotten on their feet and were trotting away, even the calf's mother.

"They must be really scared for the mother to leave her calf," Gemma said.

Ally saw three giant shapes marching across the greensward toward a flock of sheep that were scattering in all directions.

The hairy brown tarantulas stood ten feet tall.

One of the arachnids hopped thirty feet across the grass and landed on a young ewe. It lowered its massive bulk and sank its fangs into the sheep's back.

Ace approached a giant spider and opened up with his M16. The heavy barrage ripped off a thick leg. Max flanked the creature. He fired into its abdomen, puncturing its exoskeleton, commingling its internal organs into pate.

The two Eco-Marines moved in to put the spider down.

Ally watched in horror as the third tarantula went airborne and came down directly on top of Ace, knocking him to the ground. She could hear his muffled scream under the giant creature as it buried its fangs and injected him with enough poison to kill twenty men. He struggled to crawl out from under the arachnid. Ace's puffy face had swollen to twice its size as the extreme overdose of deadly venom burst through his veins, its sole mission to destroy living tissue.

It was so hideous to watch, Ally had to finally look away.

"Son of a bitch!" Max waltzed right up to the murderous spider and offloaded an entire clip. He popped the spent one out, stuffed in another flesh clip, and was so mad, he emptied 30 more rounds into the thing.

Julie and Johnny were following the last tarantula as it carried off the dead sheep toward the edge of the trees, but they couldn't shoot because the mammoth creature was heading directly at Ally and Gemma.

"Ally, back into the woods." They spun around and raced through the trees until they reached the calf. The newly born animal was trying to get to its feet, but was having a difficult time, as it was still groggy from the nymph's venom.

They could hear the spider's massive legs traipsing over the leaf-covered ground.

Ally looked over her shoulder. The spider had dropped the sheep and had set its sights on a new prey and was coming for them. Max, Johnny, and Julie were tramping through the trees after it but couldn't shoot without fear of a stray bullet hitting Gemma or herself. She turned to the veterinarian and saw the doctor trying to steady the calf and knew with stark realization that they had nowhere to run.

Suddenly, leaves came raining down on their heads. Ally looked up and saw a black creature blocking out the sun, hovering above them with bright red wings.

"Get down!" Gemma yelled.

Ally crouched next to the doctor and watched as the giant tarantula hawk alighted on the arachnid's back. The spider tried to buck the wasp off but its attacker had already hooked its claws and was delivering an incapacitating sting. It took a couple of minutes before the paralyzing venom took effect. The tarantula rolled over onto its back with its legs pointing up in the air and stopped moving. The wasp squatted over the spider's abdomen, released a single egg then flew off.

"Is the spider dead?" Ally asked.

"No. When that lava hatches, it will burrow inside the spider's abdomen and feed on the less crucial organs in order to keep the spider alive as long as possible. Later when it becomes an adult it'll eat its way out."

"That's disgusting."

"Nature's never subtle. Look on the bright side; we're still here."

"Yeah, thanks to the wasp."

"You guys all right?" Max asked as he came over. Julie and Johnny were standing by the tarantula, making sure that it wasn't going to suddenly revive and attack them.

"Yes, we're fine. Max, do you mind carrying this little guy back to its mother," Gemma said, bracing the calf so it wouldn't fall over.

"Sure." Max handed his assault rifle to Johnny. He came over and placed his arms around the calf's front and back legs and picked it up.

"I'm so sorry about Ace," Gemma said.

Max didn't say anything and trudged off with the calf.

Ally was saddened to see tears in his eyes.

24

Dillon stared up at the clock hanging on the wall above the chalkboard behind Miss Shelly's desk. Even though his teacher's last name was Green and she was married, she preferred that her students called her Miss Shelly. He wondered if the timepiece was broken, as the hour hand wasn't moving. His mom always said if you were too anxious for something to happen, it was like standing in front of the stove and waiting for a pot of water to boil. The short hand finally clicked to the next increment on the clock face.

One more hour until school was out.

He glanced over at the new girl. Her name was Amy Waters as Miss Shelly had made Amy introduce herself to the class. The newcomer was shy and nervous and had turned red as an apple when she spoke about herself.

Amy sat right across from him in the next row. She was marking her paper, putting Xs in the multiple-choice boxes that seemed like the best answer, and was almost done with her test.

Dillon didn't think it was fair for Miss Shelly to make Amy take a test on her first day but Amy didn't seem to mind and said she pretty much knew the definitions of a few sample words that were going to be on the exam.

Afraid Miss Shelly might catch him looking at Amy's paper and think he was cheating, he quickly turned back to his own test. He was almost done and knew all the words so far as he loved to read, especially when it was a DC Comic. He snuck another glance over at Amy. She had turned her test paper facedown and placed her pencil on the desk. She was sitting up straight with her fingers clasped together, facing the front of the classroom.

Five minutes later, Miss Shelly called time and told everyone to put their pencils down. Dillon had three unanswered questions left, which he didn't know but went ahead and marked off a box for each one figuring he might make a lucky guess and pick the right answer.

"I have some wonderful news, class," Miss Shelly said as she walked down a row, collecting papers. "We've just gotten a new shipment of books."

By a new shipment, Miss Shelly meant that someone from the teaching staff had gone out on a scavenger hunt and gathered up reading material from the local libraries and schools and abandoned bookstores for the students. It also meant there were boxes of books intended for the adult readers that lived in the barracks. Most of the time no one bothered to differentiate one from the other and the children and adult books were lumped together, which was exciting for the children but embarrassing for the teaching staff.

Dillon was particularly fond of the *Diary of a Wimpy Kid* series and *The Adventures of Captain Underpants* whenever he didn't have his nose pressed in a DC Kids comic book. He also liked the pictures of the animals in *National Geographic* and wondered what kind of treat the photographers gave the tigers and lions to pose for the camera.

He heard a loud snort and looked under his desk. Winston was snoring, fast asleep by his feet. Whenever Miss Shelly was teaching class, Dillon's mom would leave Winston under her care instead of taking him with her on a patrol. She told Dillon sometimes it was better Winston didn't come as it was too dangerous where they were going. Dillon knew the real reason his mom wanted Winston to stay behind was so he could protect Dillon, Miss Shelly, and the other kids in the class.

Miss Shelly collected the last of the test papers and put them on her desk. She walked over and opened the door to the adjoining room. "I want everyone to stand and file into the Reading Room, one row at a time."

Dillon and the other thirty kids jumped out of their seats and formed lines, bumping into one another, glad to be out from behind their desks.

"Today, I want the class to break up into groups of two so each student will have a reading partner," Miss Shelly said. "If you don't already have a partner in mind, don't worry, I'll pick one for you."

Dillon turned to Amy. "Want to be reading partners?"

She looked at him and half smiled. "Sure. What's your name?"

"Dillon."

"Is that your dog?"

Winston was stretching under Dillon's desk with his butt up in the air.

"Yeah. His name is Winston."

"Is he named after someone important?"

"Yeah, I think."

Dillon, Amy, and the other students marched single-file into the next room and quickly dispersed to rummage through what had to be over fifty cardboard boxes up against the walls, filled with magazines and books.

Dillon and Amy crossed the spacious room that had once been a large storeroom and went over to the boxes stacked under the window. Winston trotted right behind and found a patch of sunlight on the rug to bask in.

Opening the closed flaps of a box, Dillon looked inside, and found it filled with magazines. He dug through the pile and came upon issues of *Time*, *Newsweek*, *People*, and *Popular Mechanics,* none of which interested Dillon, though he did keep a *Popular Mechanics* that he knew his big brother, Ryan, would like to read.

Amy was hunched over a box. "This one's full of comics."

"Really?" Dillon said, excitedly.

"Come over and see."

Dillon scooted next to Amy and looked inside the box. He took out a small stack of comics and leafed through them. "Holy moly. Here's some *Pitt*."

"What's *Pitt*?"

"He's this bad ass alien dude who comes to Earth to protect this boy, Timmy."

"Did you just say, bad ass?" Amy whispered so the other kids wouldn't hear.

"Yeah, I guess I did," Dillon said and they both laughed. He kept rifling through the comics. "Look, here's some issues of *Gen13*, *Young Justice*, *The New Adventures of Superboy*, and an *Infinite Crisis* with Batman and Superman. Hey, check this out." Dillon showed Amy the front cover of a Marvel comic with Daredevil and Electra in a passionate embrace, kissing.

"Any with Barbara Gordon?" Amy asked.

"You mean, Batgirl?"

"Ah, yeah! She's my favorite."

Dillon kept looking and picked up another stack. "No, sorry, there's..." he glanced back inside the box. "Ah, you're not going to believe it. This is so cool." He reached inside and took out a 500-page Showcase volume of *Batgirl* and handed the heavy book to Amy.

"Oh my God," Amy said, opening it up and smiling as she perused the black and white frames.

Dillon browsed through more comics. "Here's some *Ball and Chain*."

"What's *Ball and Chain*?"

"It's this married couple that are always arguing and one day get superpowers. Only they don't know their powers only work when they're together. Just before they're supposed to go up against this evil villain and his minion army, they get into a silly fight and split up. Which puts them in danger as they no longer have superpowers."

"Sounds kind of sad."

"Oh my God," a girl squealed from across the room.

"Looks like someone else found what they wanted," Dillon said.

Winston had been stretched out on the rug but was suddenly on his feet, snarling.

"What is it, boy?"

More kids started to yell and scream and were backing away from the boxes.

"Everyone, go back to the classroom," Miss Shelly shouted.

"What's going on?" Amy asked Dillon.

"See for yourself." Dillon pointed to a gray creature climbing out of one of the boxes. It had two antennas and a three-foot long tapered body. Once the thing reached the carpet, it was extremely fast and wiggled across the room like a fish out of water. More and more giant silverfish came out of the boxes.

"We gotta get out of here," Amy said as the creepy bugs scurried every which way on the carpet. Winston was chasing a silverfish racing along the baseboard.

"They're not that scary," Dillon boasted.

"What do you mean?"

"You want to see Batgirl in action?" He held open his hands.

Amy gave Dillon the five-pound, 500-page book.

Dillon waited until a silverfish was close enough then tossed the book on top of the bug's back. The three filaments at the end of its abdomen continued to twitch even though the smooshed insect was clearly dead.

He reached down and picked up the book, revealing a flat metallic smudge on the carpet. He looked at Amy. "Another book-eater bites the dust."

Miss Shelly ushered most of the students into the classroom except for a few of the older boys and shut the door. She looked over at Dillon and Amy. "Amy, would you like to go back in the classroom?"

"No, Miss Shelly."

"Okay. Everyone grab a broom, anything you can find."

Dillon glanced across the room and saw Winston rolling around on his back on the remains of a dead silverfish. "Winston, stop it."

"Why is he doing that?" Amy asked.

"I don't know. Dumb dog."

The older boys were having fun, running after the scampering silverfish, and smashing them. It took maybe ten minutes before Miss Shelly called a timeout. "I think that should do it."

Dillon went over to the wash sink in the corner of the room. He pulled a couple paper towels from the dispenser, wiped off the back of Amy's book, and gave it back to her. "There, good as new."

"Thank you, Dillon. That's so sweet."

"Ugh," Dillon replied trying not to blush.

25

Cass had been drained mentally and physically. She was bone-tired from trying to make contact on the ham radio and the almost disastrous spacewalk then discovering alien life forms had tagged along and were now in the spacecraft. She'd spent almost half an hour frantically checking all over her body, and then Rob, making sure they were no longer carriers before retreating back into the Harmony module. She'd turned off Rob's power pack so that it could recharge and anchored the robonaut just outside her sleeping bay before slipping inside her bag and falling fast asleep.

Sometime during her slumber, she had a wild dream. She was alive floating out in space, and was completely naked, but couldn't feel the cold from the black void as she was drifting into the sun. Solar flares erupted from the fiery star and encompassed her body but instead of charring her flesh, the heat warmly caressed her skin.

Rob passed by her and gave her a casual wave then exploded in a ball of fire.

That was just about the time the sun became a hideous face and opened its mouth...

Cass woke up in a sweat. She unzipped her sleeping bag and wiggled out of the berth, relieved to see Rob waiting inanimately with its legs fastened to the bulkhead.

She checked her wristwatch and was surprised she had actually been asleep for more than three hours. She hadn't realized how worn-out she had become; like a car on empty, running on fumes.

Unplugging Rob's charger, she restarted its power supply and booted up its operating systems. "Hello, Rob."

Rob's head turned so its visor was facing Cass. "Hello, Cass."

It was a simple exchange and wondrous to hear even though the voice was computerized. She didn't care, as it was someone—something—she could talk to and wile away the time still afforded to her. When you were marooned out in space, you learned to accept whatever you could get.

"Let's have some lunch, shall we?"

Rob wasn't programmed to respond.

"Follow me," Cass said. She waited until Rob released its foot pegs then soared behind her through the compartment. She stopped at a shelf with various slots labeled with food names. Rob drifted beside her and anchored to the bulkhead.

She reached into a cubby and grabbed a pouch marked *Banana Nut Squash*. She inserted the tube between her lips, squeezed the bag, and sucked the bland baby food into her mouth.

Rob turned its head, and raised its right arm, pointing its index finger at the far junction. "Something has triggered my motion detectors."

"What is it?" Cass said, letting go of the pouch and leaving it to free float.

She stared down the tubular compartment but didn't see anything right away, and then a burly shape gradually appeared. It had to be close to six feet long and was floating slowly in her direction.

She had taken a couple of biology classes in college and had studied the microscopic animal and knew that it was impossible for it to grow this big.

But yet, there it was...

A tardigrade.

The conical snout looked like the end of a fire hose nozzle and was pushed into a faceless head. Its segmented body looked like a cross between loose canvas and the wrinkly skin of a Shar Pei. It had four pairs of pudgy legs and weird-looking stick-like claws for feet, and its wide girth took up almost the entire cylindrical passage.

During a drought, a tardigrade—sometimes known as a water bear—would go into cryptobiosis, a hibernation, and was so hardy it could roll up into a barrel like ball called a tun and remain dormant for more than 25 years until it came in contact with water and was rejuvenated back to an active state.

Cass had no idea how long this one had been inactive inside the space station. She figured it must have gotten wet when she spilt the water while using the ham radio but that couldn't have been what caused such an amazing transformation; certainly there had to be another reason.

Tardigrades were the most incredible creatures. They could endure extreme cold temperatures of −300 degrees and intense heat up to 300 degrees, withstand radioactivity 1,000 times over the lethal level, and even survive outer space.

Cass couldn't believe it. If things weren't bad enough, now she was trapped inside the space station with a bear-like creature that was virtually indestructible!

26

Just before impact...

"Are you sure this is the street?" Frank asked. He kept looking to his left then his right checking address signs either on the front of the houses or painted on the curb by the driveways as he slowly proceeded through the block of homes.

Wanda looked down at the slip of paper in her hand. "Not unless there're two Riversides." She gazed out the windshield. "It should be further down."

"You said a woman called?" Wade asked from the backseat of the Suburban.

"That's right."

"How do you know it's not a trap?"

"We don't," Frank replied. "But there's always that chance."

Wanda glanced at her side mirror and could see the small 14-passenger school bus following them. Crandall was behind the wheel, Jack riding shotgun in the front passenger seat behind the folding door. Whenever there was hope of finding survivors wanting to relocate, they brought the bus.

They continued down the road until it dead-ended into a cul-de-sac. The address they were looking for was the house in the middle of the horseshoe.

Frank made the half turn, stopped, and kept the motor running. "What do you think?"

"The curtains are drawn which means there may be someone hiding inside."

Wade leaned forward in his seat. "They had to have heard us pull up. Don't you think they'd be coming out?"

"Would you, if someone you didn't know showed up at your house?" Wanda asked.

"No, I guess not. You want me to go up and knock on the door?"

"Might have to," Frank said.

"I'm going with you," Wanda said and opened her door. Wade got out and cocked a round into the Remington pump. They went over, crossed the sidewalk, and headed up the walkway to the front stoop. Wade pounded his fist on the front door.

"Easy, Wade. You don't want to scare them."

"Sorry, just wanted to make sure they heard me." He leaned his head close to the door to see if he could hear anyone inside.

"Anything?"

"No. Wait a sec. I hear someone moving around in there."

"Step back! Now!"

Wanda and Wade had just sidestepped away from the door when they heard a loud blast from the other side. A bowling ball-size hole exploded out the thick door, spewing woodchips everywhere.

"We've been setup!" Frank yelled out his window. Crandall pulled the bus alongside. He left the engine running and opened the door.

Jack piled out. He was armed with a Mossberg 500 assault shotgun and had on his belt of throwing knives. He turned and saw figures running out from the side gate. "On your right!" he yelled to Wanda and Wade.

Three men with handguns ran across the brown lawn, firing their weapons. Four more came out from the opposite side of the house, two of them with automatic rifles.

Wanda spun around and shot the man closest to her. He stumbled and fell flat on his face when his knees were blown out from under him. Wade offloaded two rounds of buckshot into another man.

Frank got out of the Suburban, drew his nine-millimeter, and dropped a hostile with a headshot.

Jack fired off a shot and missed as two men came at him with revolvers. He dropped his shotgun on the ground and slightly raised his hands. The men stopped in their tracks thinking Jack was giving up. As soon as they let their guard down, Jack snatched two knives from his belt and threw them underhand. Each blade hit a man dead center in the chest. "That'll teach you to bring a gun to a knife fight," he said as they slumped to the ground.

A man with a machete lunged at Wanda while her back was turned. Wade intercepted the attacker and shot the man in the head, splattering his brains on the side of the house.

Crandall went hand-to-hand with an assailant and after a short tussle, got the man in a headlock and broke his neck.

Wade walked over and kicked in the front door. A man with a gun was sitting on the couch. A bloody knife was on the cushion next to his thigh. When he raised the muzzle of his gun, Wade shot him.

The living room looked like it had been hit by a whirlwind; furniture toppled over, magazines strewn everywhere on the carpet, breakables broken, a dead man and woman with their throats slit, lying next to the shattered glass coffee table.

"Guess we know who the woman was," Wade said as Wanda walked into the room.

"Let's go," she said and stepped outside.

"Well, that was a bust," Crandall said.

Everyone got back in their vehicles and they drove out of the cul-de-sac.

Twenty minutes later, they were back on the Golden Gate Bridge, heading back to Fort Mason. They were halfway across the span when they heard the earth-shattering boom.

Frank shot a glance to his left. "Get down!" He turned his head and leaned toward Wanda as far as possible, constrained by his seatbelt harness. Wanda raised her arms to cover her face as Wade ducked down in the back seat. The windows on the left side of the Suburban blew out, raining shards of glass into the SUV as the powerful concussion punched out the windows on the other side of the vehicle.

Crandall lost control of the bus behind them and he and Jack were pitched out of their seats when the windows shattered, sucking the oxygen out of the air.

The blast wave rammed the Suburban and bus and catapulted them across the pavement like leaves swept away in a windstorm.

27

Just before impact...

Ally felt the ground rumbling under her feet. The horses and cattle around her started to panic and ran in every direction. Flocks of sheep were scattering across the grassland. "What's happening?" she yelled.

"We're having an earthquake," Gemma shouted, trying to keep her balance.

The field started to lift in places and fissures began to open up. A few goats tried to jump over a widening crevasse but were unable to clear the gap and fell into the deep chasm, bleating all the way down.

Max, Julie, and Johnny had been trying to extricate Ace's body out from under the giant tarantula when the earth began to shake.

Before any of them knew what was happening, a powerful shockwave knocked everyone off their feet and sent them sprawling across the grass. Ally clawed her fingers into the dirt and dug the tips of her boots into the ground to stop herself from rolling. The howling wind was so loud it hurt her ears.

Smaller animals were carried off like lightweight debris caught in the grips of a twister. The ground continued to tremble wildly for more than a minute.

Ally looked up and saw the distant blue sky beyond a stand of trees turning an ashen gray. She glanced over at Gemma who was lying on her belly and saw the veterinarian staring in the same direction.

"Looks like a dust cloud," Gemma said.

"Jesus," Max said, and got on his feet. "Anyone hurt?"

Julie and Johnny stood and shook their heads.

"You two okay?"

"Yes, I think so," Gemma said and looked over at Ally as they both got up off the ground.

"I'm fine," Ally said.

"That was one heck of a shaker," Johnny said. "What would you say, a seven-point-oh on the Richter Scale?"

"Try eight or nine," Max said. No sooner had he said that, the ground beneath their feet began to jolt again, but not as forceful as the first earthquake.

They stood motionless and waited for the aftershock to subside.

Max turned to Johnny. "Go back to the ATVs and bring the one back with the longer cargo bed so we can transport Ace's body."

"Sure thing," Johnny said. He cradled his assault rifle in the crook of his arm and double-timed across the field.

"How about Julie and I lift this thing and you and Ally grab one of Ace's arms and drag him out?" Max said to Gemma.

Ally felt squeamish touching Ace. He looked like a bloated corpse that had been pulled out of the ocean, nothing like the young man she remembered.

"Are you okay, Ally?"

It took her a moment to gather her nerve. "Yes, I'm fine."

Max and Julie put down their rifles and positioned themselves, grabbing a portion of the spider's thick body, and getting ready to lift it up.

"Now!" The Eco-Marines raised the heavy spider while Gemma and Ally grabbed Ace and dragged his body out from under the creature.

"Good work," Max said as he and Julie let the spider drop to the ground. "Now all we have to do—"

"Run!" Johnny yelled as he dashed back.

"What is it?" Max shouted.

"Ants! Hundreds of them!"

Ally looked at the sloping hillside and saw giant black ants marching down.

"They must have crawled out of the ground after the earthquake," Gemma said.

"Oh no!" Julie said. She was looking in the opposite direction.

Ally turned and saw an army of giant red ants coming out of the ground.

"This is not good," Max said. "If my training serves me right, red and black ants are mortal enemies."

"Which leaves us trapped in the middle," Gemma said.

28

Just before impact...

Shelly had dismissed all of her students except for Dillon and Amy who were sitting in the back of the classroom, each reading a comic book from the short stack they had collected from the Reading Room. Winston had found another sunny spot to lie in and was enjoying a quiet afternoon nap.

Amy's mom appeared in the doorway and knocked before coming in. Shelly looked up from her desk.

"Hi. It's Debra, right?" Shelly said.

"Yes, you remembered," Debra replied with a friendly smile.

"Just a knack I have; placing a face with a name. Part of being a teacher I guess."

"So, how was Amy's first day?"

"She was a model student. Even made some friends." Shelly motioned to the back of the room where Dillon and Amy were sitting, engrossed in their newly found reading material.

"I was worried that she wouldn't fit in."

"Kids will surprise you," Shelly said.

"That's for—"

The windows exploded inward showering the room with a deadly hail of sharp glass as the walls shook and the ceiling threatened to come down. Shelly and Debra covered their faces and darted down the aisles to the back of the room. Luckily, the children hadn't been too close to the windows and had not been harmed. The overhead lights began to pop. There was a loud rumble as the building continued to shudder.

Winston yelped. A sliver of glass had struck him in the back.

While Debra made sure the kids were okay, Shelly knelt beside the injured dog, cautious at first, not knowing the extent of his pain and whether he would snap at her.

"It's okay, boy," Dillon said, once he realized that his pet had been injured.

"Debra, can you toss me that towel hanging on the wash sink?"

Amy's mom snatched up the towel and rushed over.

Shelly plucked the glass out of Winston's back and wrapped the towel around him to staunch the bleeding. "There, good as new," she said, and saw Dillon give her a brave smile.

People were yelling and screaming both inside and outside the building.

A man ran down the hall and stopped at the doorway. "Get out! You need to get to high ground!" He stormed off to warn the others.

"What do we do?" Debra asked.

"The stairs!" Shelly grabbed Winston in her arms and motioned for everyone to follow her. They were just entering the hallway when she saw a large flood racing toward them through the building, the water so high it was almost touching the ceiling.

She headed down the hall and rounded the corner, reaching the bottom step of the stairwell. "Hurry!" Grabbing the handrail with one hand, Shelly hefted the injured dog up the stairs. Dillon and Amy were right on her heels; Debra behind making sure the children didn't stumble and fall.

The flashflood rushed onto the first floor of the building in a matter of seconds and steadily rose up the stairwell. When Shelly reached the second-story landing she briefly glanced down the railing between the narrow gaps between the floors and saw the tidal water continuing to rise. "Keep going!"

Seawater splashed against the walls and surged up the steps.

Debra clambered up as fast as she could as the tidal wave caught up and swelled over her ankles and her knees, and then up to her waist. She was unable to see where she was stepping and slipped.

Dillon and Amy were only one step ahead of the torrential tide.

"Help!" Debra yelled, one hand on the railing as the swirling water sucked her under.

Shelly turned when she heard the cry and looked down. She waited a second for Dillon and Amy to catch up and put Winston down on the step. "Keep going! And help Winston up!"

Dillon didn't hesitate and pushed Amy ahead of him as he bent down and coaxed Winston up the stairs.

"Hold on, Debra!" Shelly shouted. She held onto the railing and guided herself down into the water. She could see the submerged woman's hair floating just under the surface and knew that Debra wouldn't be able to cling on for very much longer until she ran out of breath.

Shelly ducked under the water and slid her hand down the banister. Her fingers quickly felt Debra's hand and clamped around her wrist. She used all her strength and started back up the stairs, one step at a time, pulling Debra up with her. Once their heads were out of the water and they could fill their lungs with air, the ascent became easier.

Soon the flood subsided and the seawater started to retreat back down the stairs.

They finally made it up to the third-floor landing where Dillon and Amy were waiting anxiously with Winston.

"Are you kids okay?" Shelly asked, even though she was soaking wet and looked like a drowned dog.

Amy ran up and gave her mother a big hug.

They walked into the main barracks where fifty other people were congregating by the shattered windows.

Winston ran over and jumped up on a bottom bunk. Dillon and Amy sat on the mattress to comfort the dog while Shelly and Debra went over to one of the blasted-out windows to see what everyone was looking at.

The city streets of San Francisco were flooded and most of the high-rise buildings had been destroyed as well as the surrounding metropolitan areas.

Shelly was speechless, as was everyone, as they stared at the massive dust cloud blanketing out the sky on the other side of the bay.

29

Just before impact...

Ryan and Celeste were descending Mt. Hamilton Road in the Mustang when they heard a sonic boom. Seconds later the car was suddenly blown off the pavement against an embankment by a powerful gust of wind. Hitting the brakes and fighting the wheel, Ryan managed to stop or they would have plummeted down the mountain.

"What the hell was that?" Ryan asked. He turned off the engine, opened the driver's door, and stepped outside. Before Celeste got out, she grabbed a pair of binoculars off the seat.

They walked over to the edge of the road, which afforded them a good view of the valley and the countryside further north. Celeste looked through the binoculars and panned the horizon. "Oh my God!"

"What do you see?"

"A large cloud of smoke."

"From what?"

"Had to have been a meteor strike. A really big one." She continued to scan the terrain below. "There's flooding in the valley. The shock wave must have created a tsunami. All I can see are rooftops, but the flood surge seems to be receding."

"How big do you think it was?"

"Hard to say." Celeste lowered the binoculars and looked at Ryan. "I don't suppose you've ever heard of Barringer Crater?"

"No, can't say as I have.'

"It used to be a famous impact site, that is before all this started happening."

"So where is this crater?"

"Near Winslow, Arizona. The crater is almost four thousand feet in diameter and over five hundred feet deep. The impact energy to create such a crater is believed to have been ten megatons."

"Ten megatons. Are you serious?"

"That's almost a thousand times more destructive than the atomic bomb dropped on Hiroshima."

"Jesus." Ryan glanced out over the valley. "So how big do you think this one was?"

"Big enough to wipe out a city."

"Fort Mason's right on the wharf."

"Then I'd say they're in big trouble."

"We've got to get down there." Ryan dashed back and jumped behind the wheel. He fired up the engine, shifted into gear, and punched the accelerator before Celeste could even get her door all the way closed.

30

Cass watched in disbelief as the giant tardigrade started to squeeze its bulk through the hatchway coupling modules Harmony and Destiny. She didn't know if it was her imagination but the thing seemed to be continuously growing. Her greatest fear was the tardigrade would swell so large, it would block the passage and she wouldn't be able to return to the Columbus.

She tried to recall if tardigrades were considered dangerous. The one thing she did remember was everyone always thinking how adorable the microscopic creatures looked, moving about on a slide like cuddly bears under the high-powered microscope lens.

It was halfway through the hatch when Cass noticed that parts of its skin were slicing away and floating about the compartment. At first, she thought the inner edge of the metal hatchway was gouging into the tardigrade's thick-shelled body.

But as she continued to watch, she realized the creature was sloughing its protective outer shell, much like a snake sheds it skin. She wondered if this was the only time when the animal was truly vulnerable, during the ecdysis process.

The last thing she wanted was to confront the thing, but she knew she would have to make a stand if she wanted to survive and not let herself be forced into a corner where she would surely die. She couldn't remember if tardigrades breathed oxygen, but figured they must, and that a creature this size had to be depleting the reserves at a rapid rate.

She drifted backward toward the hatchway that led into the Tranquility module while Rob floated beside her like a companion taking a leisurely swim in the lake. She contemplated going into the next compartment and closing the hatch, but that meant shutting herself off from being able to access food, water, and the ham radio.

No, she was going to have to find a way to dissuade the steadily advancing tardigrade. She glanced around for some sort of weapon that she could improvise but there wasn't anything within reach. Perhaps she could order Rob to intercede but had no idea how she would instruct the robonaut to try and kill the living creature.

Just as she was about to give up hope, something caught her eye. It was gangly and gold-colored. She saw another appendage reach over and touch the tardigrade's back. Then a yellowish head with eight eyes came into view. The giant spider climbed onto the tardigrade—it looked exactly like the one Cass had seen in the laboratory.

But how was that even possible?

The arachnid found a bare spot where the hard shell had fallen off and buried its fangs into the tardigrade's soft flesh. The spider's head bobbed as it pumped its prey with its venomous poison.

The magnificent water bear shuddered and rolled upside down.

Clambering over its kill, the enormous spider kicked off with its rear legs. The movement did two things; it caused the upturned tardigrade to drift away, and propelled the spider at Cass. She could see its vicious fangs as the mouth opened. She tried to shove herself out of the way but there was nothing to push off from. All she could do was raise her arms and duck away in a last-ditch effort to protect herself as the...

Rob catapulted off the padded bulkhead like a torpedo with one arm extended straight out like Superman flying through the air.

The arachnid was caught completely by surprise, especially when Rob thrust its hand and arm down its gullet. The gigantic spider bit down on the robonaut's arm with its deadly fangs. Unaffected by the venom, Rob churned its arm inside the spider's body like it was making butter and eviscerated the internal organs. The spidery legs went limp like bent tree branches floating underwater.

Cass had to shield her face from the liquids. She couldn't tell if the droplets were blood or lethal venom but wasn't taking any chances. When Rob pulled out its arm, the appendage was covered with green slime and gore.

At first, Cass was speechless and completely blown away at what she had just witnessed, but then she finally found the words. "Thank you, Rob."

"You are welcome, Cass."

31

When Frank regained consciousness, he was surprised to find himself hanging upside down by his seatbelt harness. He looked over and saw Wanda, unconscious, suspended with her arms bent and her hair draped on the headliner.

"Jesus, what just hit us?" Wade said from the back seat.

"I'm not sure," Frank replied, reaching up and unsnapping his seatbelt. He slid awkwardly off the seat and shimmied out through the window. He caught a glimpse of his reflection in the side mirror. His face was pocked with tiny red gashes made by the flying shards of safety glass.

He got to his feet and rushed around the front of the overturned Suburban to the passenger side. He reached in, undid Wanda's seatbelt, and made sure she didn't fall on her head and break her neck when she came down. He grabbed her arms and carefully pulled her out.

"Wanda! Can you hear me?"

Wade crawled out the back. "Is she hurt?" he asked.

"I'm not sure," Frank said and dropped to his knees next to his wife. He put his head down by her face to see if she was breathing and felt a faint puff of air against his cheek. He tried to wake her up by gently shaking her shoulder.

Wanda slowly opened her eyes. "What just happened?"

"Thank God you're okay." Frank glanced across the wide span of asphalt and saw a massive gray cloud beyond the suspension cables, covering the eastern foothills of Berkeley. He looked down at Wanda. "A meteor took out the East Bay."

"Holy shit!" Wade yelled.

Frank stood and helped Wanda up. They followed Wade over to the school bus, which appeared to have tumbled a few times as the roof was crumbled and the side was smashed in. The vehicle was resting up against the cement barrier that ran along the side of the bridge. Scores of other abandoned cars and trucks had been picked up and tossed across the roadway like a bunch of Tonka toys.

Wade climbed up onto the battered hood and got down on his hands and knees so he could see inside.

"Are they okay?" Frank asked.

"Give me a second," Wade answered and climbed through the smashed-out windshield.

Frank could hear Wade moving about inside the bus. A minute later, Crandall's head popped out of the opening. His face was cut up like everyone else. He managed to squeeze his big frame out and scooted down off the hood. He made a face when his boots hit the pavement and grabbed his shoulder.

"Are you badly hurt?" Frank asked.

"I think I dislocated my shoulder. Just give me a sec." Crandall went over to the side of the bus, took a deep breath, and slammed his shoulder into the hard metal. He let out a grunt and smiled at Frank. "There, right as rain."

Wade crawled out of the bus and slid down on the asphalt. "Crandall, where's Jack?"

"What, he's not in there?"

"No."

"You don't think he was thrown out of the bus?" Wanda said.

"Let's hope not." Frank and the others made their way over to the railing.

"Oh my God," Wanda said. "There he is."

Jack was dangling below, fifty feet down off the side of the bridge. His right arm was entwined in a tattered length of silk still attached to what was left of a spider web and was the only thing keeping him from falling the rest of the way down to the ocean. The channel below was filled with floating debris, capsized sailboats, and even cars, destroyed structures ripped from their foundations by the flood and smashed apart like balsa kindling.

"Jack! Can you hear me?" Wade hollered down.

Jack looked up. "Hey, there!"

"Hold on. We're going to pull you up." Frank turned and yelled over to Crandall, "Grab the rope out of the Suburban."

Crandall dashed over to the wrecked truck.

"Maybe we could snare that webbing and pull him up," Wade said.

"That stuff's like crazy glue."

Crandall came back with a large coil of repelling line, and a semiautomatic pistol tucked in his belt. He'd also grabbed two assault rifles. He handed one gun to Frank and the other to Wanda. He tied off one end of the rope to the railing and threw the rest down to Jack.

"Tie it around your waist," Crandall instructed.

Jack grabbed the end, looped it around his midsection, and cinched a knot with one hand as his other hand was trapped in the webbing. Suspended by the rope, Jack was finally able to use one of his knives from his belt, and began sawing away at the thick, silk strand.

The vibration drew three orb weaver spiders out from the bridge's understructure.

"Jack! Stop cutting!" Frank yelled.

Wanda aimed her rifle at the spiders. "I can't get a clear shot without hitting Jack."

"Give me your weapon," Wade said. "I think I can pick one off from here."

Wanda turned and tossed her rifle to Wade, who caught it, and immediately lined up his shot. He fired off a short burst. The bullets ripped through the giant spider's body, exploding it like a limejuice-filled water balloon.

Another orb weaver crept toward Jack, and was only a couple feet away from its prey, when Frank got off a quick round and obliterated the arachnid, severing three of its legs and causing it to detach from the web and plummet to a watery grave.

"I'm loose!" Jack yelled up.

Frank handed his rifle to Wanda and helped Crandall hoist Jack up.

Wade fired off a few more shots at the remaining spider, scaring it back under the bridge.

Once Jack was free of the strong adhesive, the group decided to climb over the center divider barrier to the pedestrian walkway on the opposite side of the span to get a better look at the devastation.

"Oh my God," Wanda gasped when they reached the fencing and gazed out.

Frank put his arm around Wanda as she began to cry.

A flood surge was flowing out of San Francisco and retreating back into the bay. It reminded Frank of the horrific news coverage he'd once seen when an unstoppable 23-foot tsunami devastated a coastal city in northern Japan.

"There's no way... they could... have survived," Wanda said in between sobs.

Frank wanted to comfort her and tell her not to give up hope.

But he knew she was right: No one in Fort Mason could have escaped that.

32

The terrifying drive up to the observatory wasn't half as bad as coming down the mountain. Each time they came to a sharp curve, Ryan was tempted to stare out through the windshield at the sprawling terrain below. Instead he kept his eyes on the winding road and tried not to get distracted by his peripheral vision.

He'd been riding the pedal and could smell the brake pads. Twice he saw Celeste lean toward him, afraid to look out her window as if she might fall into the abyss. He knew exactly how she felt, as he had that hollow feeling in his stomach he often got when flying in an airplane.

They came down a short grade and his ears popped. He hadn't realized the difference in atmospheric pressure until now. He opened his mouth and yawned, clearing his ears even more.

For the next forty-five minutes, Ryan tackled the hazardous roads, crossing the next mountain down to the outskirts of San Jose before stopping almost at the base of the foothills.

Even though some of the floodwaters had retreated back to the San Francisco Bay, there was still standing water in the streets. It was impossible to determine how deep the water was unless there was something visible like a partially submerged car or a traffic sign. Most of the streets looked impassable.

"Maybe we should have stayed on the other side of the mountain and found another way," Ryan said.

"Well, we're here now," Celeste said, her tone suggesting that she had no desire to return back up the mountain. "There has to be someway we can go."

"I really want to get back to the city. See if everyone's okay."

"Let's see if we can get to the Dish. We can call Fort Mason on the landline."

"All right." Ryan scanned the streets below, and after some consideration, chose a stretch of flooded roadway the low-frame Mustang might be able to drive through. He knew if the water got too deep it would enter the tailpipe, and once the pressure of the exhaust wasn't unable to push the water out, the engine would stall and they would be stranded.

"Cross your fingers," Ryan said. He drove down the hill and slowly entered a stream that ran between a neighborhood of houses. The front of the Mustang dipped slightly as the water level got higher. He lowered his side window and looked out. The murky water was a third of the way up the door.

Ryan pushed down on the accelerator and gunned the Mustang. He prayed the water didn't get any deeper and that they didn't hit a submerged object that might tear up the undercarriage.

The muscle car moved along like an improvised watercraft and finally emerged on a dry stretch of roadway and then onto an overpass that crossed over the freeway.

Celeste looked out her side window at the abandoned wrecks on the freeway that were piled up by the flashflood. "There's no way we'd be able to make it down the 101."

After some navigating and considerable luck, Ryan found an onramp that took them onto Interstate 280, which wasn't flooded. Junk cars blocked most of the lanes, but Ryan was able to cut a path between and around them.

Twenty minutes later, Ryan and Celeste were back at the Dish. An Eco-Marine greeted them at the front entrance. They went inside and found Milt sitting at the console with his headphones on. He turned in his chair and slipped his headphones down around his neck. "Good, you're here."

"Do you still have contact?" Celeste asked, sitting in the chair next to Milt.

"Yes, I have Flight Engineer Cass Freeman on the radio now. She's the only remaining survivor on the International Space Station."

"My God, it's a miracle she's still alive."

"I'll put her on speaker," Milt said, and turned a switch on the console. He picked up the microphone. "Cass, can you hear me? This is Milt Tabors again."

"Yes, your signal's a five."

Milt looked over at Celeste. "Cass said they had to make repairs to their antenna and this is the best signal strength we can expect."

"You said 'they.' I thought she was the only one alive up there?"

"Technically, she is. She's managed to program a robonaut to help her."

Ryan leaned against the console and crossed his arms as he listened in.

Celeste picked up the mike. "This is Celeste Starr of the Astronomical Consortium."

"It's so good to hear your voice. You might say I've been going a little buggy up here."

"I can only imagine."

"No, I mean I literally have a bug problem. Rob, my robonaut, had to kill a giant spider. I have no idea how it could have gotten so big."

"Are any of the alien life forms inside the space station?"

"Yes."

"How did they get in?"

"We accidentally brought them in after we returned from our spacewalk to repair the antenna."

"Do you have any other insects in the lab?"

"Yes. There are ants and fruit flies."

"Kill them immediately. If they eat the life forms they'll grow as big as that spider."

"What if I ingest a life form?"

"You needn't worry. We don't know why, but for some strange reason they've only been transforming insects. Every time one of those meteorites strikes Earth, they unleash the life forms. We've been fighting giant bugs ever since."

"That's incredible."

"That's not the half of it. We've been hit pretty hard by these meteor strikes."

"Is that why all of the major cities have gone dark?"

"Almost everyone is dead."

For a moment no one spoke.

"I thought it was bad up here. This asteroid belt has destroyed just about every satellite up here. We're holding on by a thread."

"Have you seen Mother Lode? It's what we're calling the biggest asteroid."

"Yes. We should be passing..."

Celeste waited for Cass to come back.

"Cass, can you hear me?" Celeste asked. She glanced up at Ryan with a worried look on her face.

"Try her again," Ryan said.

Milt shook his head. "Don't bother. We've lost the signal."

Ryan walked across the room. He picked up the landline receiver off the cradle on the desk and dialed the number he had for contacting Fort Mason. He couldn't tell if the line was dead or if no one was picking up. He glanced over at Celeste and Milt and saw they were both staring at him.

"There's no answer."

33

Ally wasn't sure which way to run as she looked over at Gemma, Max, and Julie who were backing toward her as the horde of giant black ants made its way down the hillock. Dirt mounds were appearing on one side of the pastureland as more black ants pushed their way out of the ground. They varied in size, the larger ones as big as a medium-size car, others half as big. Their numbers were steadily increasing and soon they had become a small army.

She turned in the other direction and saw the swarm of giant red ants coming at them. "What do we do?"

"Head for those trees!" Max yelled. But as soon as they started to run toward the small grove of oaks, a band of black ants came out from between the thick trunks to cut them off.

"Which way now?" Gemma shouted.

"Maybe we can hide in that gully," Julie said and pointed to a narrow depression twenty feet away that might have been caused by the recent earthquake or natural erosion over time.

"It might be our only chance," Max said.

Ally dashed over with the others and got down inside the ditch. It was just wide enough for her to lie down on her back next to Julie while Max and Gemma slid in on their backs with the soles of their boots touching Ally and Julie's. The Eco-Marines pointed their assault rifles at the sky.

The ground trembled as if they were experiencing another aftershock but it was the rumble of the battling giant ants converging in a skirmish. Larger ants straddled the furrow and formed a bridge so their comrades could crawl over their backs. The mute warriors clacked their mandibles and butted heads as they clambered over one another.

Ally could see the smaller red ants double-teaming the larger black ants, even attacking them from behind.

The manic battle was vicious—unlike anything Ally had ever seen—as each frantic ant tried to immobilize its opponent with its deadly stinger or sever a head or a leg with its razor sharp jaws. The fury of clashing bodies started to pile up over the narrow trench.

When one of the black ants pushed its head down, sensing that there was easier prey to be found below the carnage, Max opened up with his assault rifle and riddled its exoskeleton. The dead ant collapsed across the fissure.

Soon the sky was no longer visible, blocked out by the thatching of dead ants, but still Ally could hear the battle ensuing above ground.

"What now?" Gemma whispered loud enough for everyone to hear.

"We wait it out," Max said.

An hour went by before the battle ended.

Max rolled over on his stomach and got into a kneeling position then gradually stood, all the time pushing up through the entwined limbs and heavy bodies. He managed to make a hole large enough to climb up through and helped Gemma out.

Ally crawled out, followed by Julie.

"Wow, will you look at that," Max said.

A hundred giant red ants lay dead on the battleground, mingled with an equal amount of larger black ants, each brutally slain, a few still twitching.

It had been a brutal fight to the death and looked like a gruesome scene straight out of a science fiction movie.

"We better leave. Probably not a good idea to be out in the open," Max said.

Ally couldn't wait to get back to Fort Mason.

At least they would be safe there.

34

Cass heeded Celeste's warning and set out to kill the colony of ants and the remaining fruit flies. She decompressed the ant farm containment and watched the tiny insects shrivel and die through the Plexiglas. Then she hooked up a hose from a liquid nitrogen tank to an adapter on the side of the other habitat and froze the fruit flies to death. She didn't relish her next task but knew a quick death was better than an agonizing slow demise from starvation and euthanized the lab rats and guinea pigs.

She drifted out of the Columbus module through the hatchway into Harmony sleeping quarters and then into Destiny where Rob was corralling the giant tardigrade and spider by the entrance hatch to the Quest airlock.

Cass wasn't taking a chance and wore a surgical mask, as there were still liquid droplets floating about the compartment. She still had no idea if the green goblets were insectaria blood or deadly venom. She didn't mind being up close to the tardigrade, as it looked harmless, especially as it was dead. But the spider was another story. Dead or not, the arachnid was hideous. The last thing she wanted was to have to touch it.

She was more than grateful to give Rob the honors.

"Rob, open the hatch."

The robonaut gave the hovering creatures each a gentle nudge to keep them in place and turned around. It spun the wheel on the hatch and pulled open the door.

"Rob, place the cargo into the equipment airlock."

The tardigrade was the first to go in. It was a tight fit at first, but Rob managed to squeeze it through. The robonaut pushed the spider in next.

"Seal the hatch."

Rob complied with the command.

Cass manned the controls and depressurized the airlock and opened the outer door. "How about we give our uninvited guests a fond farewell?"

Rob didn't respond.

"Follow me," Cass instructed and drifted into the next module. Rob followed close behind. Cass stopped herself and gazed out the center portal of the cupola and was relieved to see the two bizarre creatures floating away out in space.

"Time to gear up," Cass said.

Though she hadn't been looking forward to another spacewalk, Cass knew she had no choice as the only way off the space station was piloting the Soyuz, and that meant removing the asteroid that was blocking the passageway to the spacecraft. It was risky at best and might not even produce positive results. For all she knew, the asteroid had punched a hole in the hull and was the only thing sealing the breach. Once the asteroid was removed a leak could cause the structure to rupture and then she would be worse off than when she started.

The only way she would know for sure was to go out there and see for herself.

She got back into her Extravehicular Mobility Unit with Rob's assistance, and afterward, the two of them were outside again, navigating in space. Cass made sure their tethers were securely fastened and glided along the closest truss until her helmet lights shined on a bulge above the Soyuz coupler.

The asteroid had a rough surface and was twice the size of a large medicine ball.

Cass took a pry bar from her tool belt. Rob already had a similar implement in its hand. "Rob, place the end of your tool under the rock." She waited for Rob, and when he was ready, she stuck the tip of her pry bar under her side of the asteroid. "Now push down!"

Their joint effort resulted in dislodging the meteor chunk from the concavity.

Cass half-expected a pressurized gush but the hull seemed intact. It reminded her of when she would go grocery shopping and grab a food can from the shelf only to find that it was dented, and then would quickly put it back, afraid she would get botulism from the contents if there was an air leak in the can.

The next thing was to go back inside the space station, program Rob, and give the robonaut its next assignment and extend the internal wall out, where it had been pushed in from the asteroid to make enough room so Cass could slide through into the Soyuz.

A feat that seemed easy enough—in theory.

It would be like taking a piece of bent metal and trying to restore it back to its original shape.

Sometimes it bent back fine.

Other times, the piece broke in half.

Cass could only pray that everything worked out for the best.

35

Frank and Wanda followed Crandall, Wade, and Jack down the embankment that skirted the three-tiered brick fortification tucked under the southern span of the Golden Gate Bridge. Over a century-and-a-half old, Fort Point had originally been built as a cannon battery to protect the bay from invading enemy ships. The once-historical site was now a ruin of toppled masonry in part from time and natural erosion, but mostly as a result of the destructive force of the powerful tsunami.

Everywhere Frank looked there were huge mounds of debris from the hundreds of houses near the marina that had been swept off their foundations. The trek back to Fort Mason wouldn't be easy. There were no roadways to follow, nothing but obstacles that needed to be averted or scaled. Mason Street and Marina Boulevard were no longer definable, buried under mud and rubble. The once pleasant four-mile walk by Crissy Field and through the Mariana District was now an arduous hike through the worst hell imaginable.

There was no telling how many bodies lie under all the detritus and rubbish.

He glanced over at Wanda and it pained him to see how haggard she looked from being so distraught, not knowing if Dillon or Ally were even alive. He wanted so much to hold her and reassure her that they were safe, and soon they would all be reunited, but the more he tried to convince himself, the less he believed it was even true.

It was doubtful that anyone could have survived such a disaster.

Jack and Crandall continued to assume the lead, Wade following behind, their rifles slung over their shoulders as they traipsed in shin-high mud, blazing a route through heaps of roofing material and demolished lumber. Automobiles were stacked on top of each other, angled in every which direction, some upside down on their roofs like a toddler's discarded toys.

Crandall glanced back at Frank. "How you two doing?"

"We're okay," Frank replied, even though he knew Wanda was far from okay.

"Watch yourselves. It's not very stable," Jack called down, climbing on top of what looked like the remnants of a shipwreck that had dashed upon the rocks and washed ashore in a collective heap.

Frank gave Jack a wave and glanced over at Wanda. "You go up first."

Wanda paused at the base of the rubble. She didn't look up, but instead, stared indecisively down at her boots.

"Honey, we have to keep going."

"I know. I'm just afraid what we might find once we get there."

"Here, let me—"

"Look out!" Crandall yelled.

Frank and Wanda gazed up.

"Oh my God!" Wanda gasped.

Jack screamed as a giant California forest scorpion hoisted him in the air and tightened its claws around his midsection. Wade stepped back and lost his footing, sliding halfway back down before catching his fall.

Crandall slid his gun strap off his shoulder and aimed his assault rifle at the creature.

"Careful, Crandall," Frank yelled. "Or you might hit Jack." He couldn't believe the size of the thing. It looked like something out of a Ray Harryhausen movie, only this wasn't a stop-motion animated clay model; this thing was real and had to be twenty feet long. It was the biggest transmogrified scorpion Frank had ever seen. He wondered if it was possible for it to have ingested more than one life form, and if it had, could that have been the reason for its immense size.

The predatory arachnid clambered over shaky rubble on its six legs, snapping its huge claw at Crandall as it pulled Jack away, trapped in the other pincher. It raised its tail high above its body, ready to strike at anything that tried to steal away its captured prey.

Frank could tell by the grimaced look on Jack's face that he was having trouble breathing and that the vise-like claw was probably crushing his ribs.

Wanda surprised him and began scaling the rickety heap.

"What are you doing?" he asked.

"I'm going to distract it," she replied and kept climbing.

Jack screamed again but this time his head slumped on his chest. If they didn't act quickly it would be too late.

Frank took another way up to further confuse the creature. It was difficult to get a proper foothold, as his weight would cause a board to break or slip out from under him and he would have to scramble for another secure position. The last thing he needed was to fall and get impaled on a split board jutting up from the ground.

Wade was doing his best to get back up and help his friend, but the mud-slick slope of debris was getting the better of him and he kept slipping.

The giant scorpion stepped sideways when it saw Wanda. It curled its tail and pointed its deadly stinger.

Wanda had created enough of a distraction for Crandall to come up from behind and fire off a short eviscerating burst into the scorpion's abdomen. The creature's legs buckled and it crashed down.

Crandall made sure it was dead and shot it twice in the head.

Scampering up, Frank reached Wanda, and the two of them managed to pry the claw open and release Jack. Miraculously, he was still alive.

"Jack, can you hear me?" Frank said.

"Yeah. Man, what the hell?"

Wade finally made it up and looked down at his friend. "Shit, Jack, you got more lives than a frigging cat."

They waited until Jack felt up to traveling and continued on.

It took them another hour before they reached the high ground at the edge of Fort Mason. The recently erected fence was flattened, so they stepped over it and made their way down Great Meadow, careful not to slip on the mud-soaked grass.

Both of the pavilions had been destroyed, leaving only the piers left.

Only one of the barracks remained standing.

They stepped down off the retaining wall into the parking lot littered with wrecked cars and trucks. Wading through the remaining standing water, Frank looked up at the barracks and could see faces staring down from the third story windows.

Shelly waved and yelled down. "Thank God you all made it back."

Crandall smiled up at his wife.

Frank was happy to see the relieved look on Wade's face when Debra and Amy waved from a window.

"Is Dillon with you?" Wanda yelled up.

"Yes, he's fine," Shelly replied.

Frank heard the drone of approaching engines and turned. Four ATV's came down Great Meadow and stopped short of the retaining wall.

Max, Julie, Gemma, and Ally climbed off the four-wheel bikes.

Wanda turned to Frank and almost collapsed in his arms.

"See," Frank said with a sigh of relief. "I told you everything would be fine."

36

Celeste had just gotten off the radio after a lengthy discussion with Cass on the International Space Station. The astronomer sat back in her chair and stared blankly at the dials and meters on the console. Sitting next to her, Milt was too stunned for words.

Finally, Ryan broke the silence. "Do you realize what you're asking her to do?"

"I'm quite aware."

"It's bad enough she's marooned up there. Now you're sending her on a suicide mission?"

Celeste turned and stared up at Ryan. "I know, it's a shit thing to ask, but what choice do we have. I've consulted the Astronomical Consortium and they all agree there's no other way. If we don't move Mother Lode out of Earth's orbital ring, the asteroid will eventually reach orbital decay."

"You're sure about that?"

"It's only a matter of time. And yes, Ryan, I'm sure," Celeste said, wiping a tear from her cheek. "What kind of a monster do you think I am?"

Ryan suddenly felt like a heel and bowed his head for a moment. He looked up apologetically. "I'm sorry. I just hate to see her put in this situation."

"So do I, but like I said before, it's this or we wait for the doomsday bomb to come crashing down."

Humans had been sacrificing their lives for centuries so that others might live. It was a gallant creed honored by the few for the many. Ryan knew Celeste was right.

"What now?" he asked.

"It's going to be dark in a couple hours. If you don't want to drive up to Mt. Hamilton in the dark, I suggest we leave now."

"Seriously? We're going back up to the observatory?"

"It's the only way we'll know if Cass was successful."

"Then we better get going," Ryan said.

***

Once when Ryan was younger, the family had driven down to Los Angeles and visited Griffith Park Observatory. Ryan had been jazzed as he wanted to boast to his friends that he had been in the same spot James Dean had fought another teenager in the scene from the movie, *Rebel Without a Cause*. The actor had been such a cultural icon they'd even put a bust of James Dean on the exact location.

Ryan remembered sitting in the planetarium and staring up at the massive ceiling while a narrator—accompanied by a background of dramatic classical music—spoke about the constellations. It all seemed so real and mind-boggling as a kid. He was a little disappointed when his mom explained that it was all a show. Even still, it was quite impressive.

But it didn't hold a candle to standing on top of Mt. Hamilton in the middle of the night. The haze had cleared and there wasn't a cloud in the sky. Even though it was extremely cold and he could feel the chill under a thick layer of clothes and a heavy parka, Ryan preferred to be outside at the moment.

He'd never seen so many stars in his life; millions of tiny pinpricks of light scattered on a magnificent black canvas. Standing over 4,000 feet above sea level, he felt like he could reach up and poke each one.

It really was like being on top of the world.

He wondered where Cass was, up there in the mix of everything.

Ryan went down the walkway and up the steps into the main building.

A small group of researchers and astronomers were clustered around the giant telescope as he came into the cavernous observation room. Some had gone up onto the catwalk. Ryan looked up and saw the end of the telescope pointing out through the narrow opening in the dome.

As the 40-ton telescope was stationary, the floor had to be raised to accommodate Celeste so she could see through the lens. The scientists had been at it most of the night, taking turns so as not to get eyestrain and miss sighting the International Space Station whenever it would make its brief orbital pass through space and could be seen by the powerful telescope.

Celeste moved away from the lens as another person took her place.

"Well?" Ryan asked as she came over to where he was standing.

"So far, she's been able to reposition the space station and align it in the orbital path with Mother Lode. That was over an hour ago. We can only hope she has enough fuel in the thrusters to complete the job."

"You look tired. Let's go grab some coffee."

They left the observation room and went down the hall. A coffee pot was brewing on a counter in the old gift shop. The hanging clothes and other souvenirs had been moved and stacked against the far end of the room so tables and chairs could be brought in, converting the space into a break room.

Ryan poured them both cups while Celeste sat down.

"Here," Ryan said, placing Celeste's coffee in front of her. "Black, right?"

"The stronger, the better."

Ryan sat across from Celeste. He sipped his coffee slowly even though it wasn't particularly hot, just something to wile away the time.

They heard heavy footsteps out in the hall. One of the researchers appeared in the doorway. "Celeste! She did it!"

"Oh my God!" Celeste said, jumping up from the table and spilling her coffee.

Celeste bolted out the door and ran back with the other man to the observation room while Ryan remained in his chair. He could hear people cheering, their howls echoing in the huge room down the hall.

It seemed that Cass had indeed, saved the planet.

Mother Lode was no longer a threat.

But as much as Ryan wanted to rejoice, he couldn't help thinking of Cass up there, dying alone, entombed in that spacecraft endlessly drifting in the eternal nothingness of space.

The landline phone rang on the service counter.

Ryan debated if he should pick it up knowing that there was also another phone in the observatory sharing the same line. But with all the hollering going on and everyone cheering, he doubted if anyone could hear it ringing.

He got up from the table, went over, and picked up the receiver. "Hello?"

"I need to talk to Celeste! Right away!"

"Milt?"

"Yeah, is this Ryan?"

"It is. What's up?"

"You got a pen handy?"

"Wait a sec." Ryan spotted a stack of Lick Observatory stationary pads and a round tin with pens on the countertop. He grabbed a note pad and pen. "Okay, I'm ready."

Milt rattled off a series of latitude and longitude coordinates. Once he was through, he asked Ryan to read it back, which he did.

"I'll make sure she gets it," Ryan said.

"No!" Milt shouted into the phone. "You need to get to that location quick!"

"Why, what's so urgent?"

When Milt told him, Ryan dropped the phone and dashed out of the room.

37

Ryan thought Celeste was out of her mind trying to tackle Mt. Hamilton Road in the middle of the night. It was harrowing enough driving the treacherous road during the day, not knowing if any moment he would cut a corner too close and send them soaring over the edge.

But that wasn't the case as he soon discovered traversing down the perilous mountain. As there were no other lights illuminating the road, the terrain beyond the reach of the Mustang's headlights was lost in the darkness, eliminating that panicky sense of vertigo he had experienced before so there was less distraction, like a horse wearing blinders.

For over three hours they drove: navigating the mountain roads and eventually through the passable city streets of San Jose to Interstate 280 and north to Highway 92 where they crossed over another mountain range into Half Moon Bay, only to find that the coastal town had been ravaged by the tsunami tidal waters.

Ryan gunned the Mustang up Highway 1 on the muddy tarmac, dodging stalled vehicles and trees ripped from their roots, partially blocking the two-lane road. He checked the clock on the dash. They had another two hours or so before daybreak.

Celeste had the dome light on so she could consult the map on her lap she had marked up before they left. "Up ahead should be Princeton Harbor."

"You honestly think there'll even be a boat we can use?"

"Let's hope so."

Ryan turned left off the highway and followed a road that curved down to a structure that had been demolished at the entrance to a long pier. Even in the dark and fog, Ryan could see sailboats and fishing trawlers that had been stripped from their dock moorings, smashed upon the boulders of Pillar Point, the outer breakwater jetty meant to protect the harbor but unable to hold back the devastating high wave of the tidal surge.

"Now what?" Ryan stopped the car. He kept the headlights on and climbed out. The mist was cool on his face and he zipped up his parka.

Celeste got out on her side. She walked around to the front of the car and stared out over the pier. "Ryan, I see a boat with some people onboard."

Ryan saw a small crew moving about on a fishing trawler. "Come on!" he shouted and they ran down the wharf.

When they were almost to the boat they heard a man on the bow yell out, "I wouldn't come any closer!" Ryan could see that he was holding a rifle. In his excitement, he hadn't thought to grab a weapon from the backseat though he had his sidearm strapped on his belt. He knew if he reached for it, the man could easily gun him down.

Rather than use force, Celeste chose a more diplomatic approach and explained why they had traveled to the harbor and how they desperately needed the fisherman's help. As soon as he heard the reason for her request, he immediately invited them to come aboard.

"Welcome aboard the *Maggie Bell*. I'm Kevin Price." After Ryan and Celeste properly introduced themselves, Kevin explained that he was the captain of the fishing trawler and that his wife, Maggie, and their son, Donny, had been crabbing twenty miles offshore when the tsunami hit so they were able to ride it out on the open waves.

"You were lucky," Ryan said, standing in the pilothouse with Celeste and Maggie. Donny was outside looking over the bow, ready to signal his father if he saw anything in the water that might damage the trawler's hull.

"Wish I could say the same for the others." Kevin turned the helm when Donny pointed off the portside. Ryan looked out the porthole and saw what looked like a capsized sailboat floating by.

"So, have you been living on your boat?" Celeste asked Maggie.

The woman looked to her husband. "What's it been, now? Six months?"

"Closer to seven," Kevin replied. "We have a portable desalination unit so fresh water hasn't been a problem though we have to go sparingly. You've heard that expression 'there's plenty of fish in the sea' so we've been able to sustain ourselves with our catches. Rock cod and lingcod mostly, and anything we pull up in our crab pots."

Ryan looked out the front window of the pilothouse and saw Donny duck as a wave washed up over the bow.

"It's going to get a little choppy," Kevin said as the boat lifted up a few feet and slammed down. The vessel continued to rise and dip in the swells like a short-circuited elevator car unable to make up its mind.

The ocean ahead was an undulating dark blue dappled with thousands of white caps. The unsettling motion was making Ryan seasick.

Maggie must have seen it in his face and handed him a cup of water and a couple of pills. "Here, swallow these."

Ryan gave her a weak smile and washed the pills down. The water helped with the nausea. He hoped the medication kicked in quick as he didn't' relish the idea of being on deck, puking his guts out over the side, especially in rough waters.

The journey out to sea took them two hours before they arrived at the Farallon Islands, which were 32 miles directly off the coast from the Golden Gate Bridge.

"Sailors used to call them the "Devil's Teeth Islands" because the waters around them are so treacherous," Kevin said, sounding like a charter boat tour guide.

Ryan had to admit the islands looked uninviting with their sheer cliffs and steep rocky shorelines. The slopes were crowded with seabird colonies, the granite stained white with guano. Large groups of seals and sea lions were gathered together, resting on the boulders at the water's edge. Even inside the pilothouse, Ryan could hear the pounding waves.

Donny waved and motioned for everyone to come out and join him on the bow.

Reluctantly, Ryan followed Maggie and Celeste out onto the deck. They grabbed the railing and looked over the side.

Ryan saw an immense fish glide alongside the trawler's hull.

"That's a great white. Twenty-footer," Donny shouted.

Celeste had taken a pair of binoculars from the pilothouse and was staring up into the morning sky that was turning a golden salmon as the easterly sun began to crown. She looked down at her watch then gazed back at the sky. After a moment, she shouted, "I think I see it!"

Maggie and Donny looked up.

It took a few seconds before Ryan saw the single parachute.

Kevin stared up through the front window of the pilothouse and changed course.

Everyone watched as the escape capsule drifted down and splashed into the sea.

Donny slipped on a pair of thick gloves and climbed over the side onto a narrow platform as the trawler maneuvered to the floating spacecraft.

Ryan could see Russian lettering on the exterior.

The young man slid down and climbed onto the bobbing escape module. He gazed through the porthole. "I see someone. She's alive!"

"Thank God," Celeste said.

Donny opened the hatch.

Cass Freeman poked her head out. Her face was haggard and her hair was greasy and she looked like she was in serious need of a bath, but she still managed to give everyone a great big smile.

"Welcome home," Celeste shouted down.

Donny helped Cass out of the hatch. Maggie had gone to relieve Kevin at the helm so he could assist Ryan as they pulled the astronaut on board. Cass's legs were too weak from spending so much time in zero gravity that she couldn't stand on her own. The boat pitched as the men tried to keep their balance and carry Cass into the pilothouse and below deck to the berthing compartment.

Once they'd put Cass on a bunk and covered her with a blanket, Celeste had to ask the burning question. "How in the world did you do it? We saw you from our observatory, pushing Mother Lode off into space."

"That wasn't me you saw. It was Rob. I programmed the robonaut to pilot the Zveza as its thrusters had the most fuel. When I saw that it was working, I made a quick call to you guys."

"That's when you gave Milt your landing coordinates."

"Yeah, I figured it was the closest spot. Luckily, I was able to squirm my way into the Soyuz descent module."

"I have to say, you're one amazing woman," Ryan said.

"You don't think I could trouble anyone for a cup of hot tea?"

"Coming right up," Maggie said and headed off to the galley.

Ryan and Celeste sat side by side on the opposite bunk.

"So," Cass said. "What's been going on down here?"

"Plenty," Ryan said, and before he knew it, he and Celeste were swapping horror stories with Cass like three long-lost friends.

38

Twenty years later...

Frank stood at the front window and peeked out through the curtain. "She's just pulling into the driveway." He kept watching as Wanda got out of her Jeep and headed for the porch steps. "Everybody hide!"

He dashed over and joined Dillon and Amy who were crouched behind the sofa with their five-year-old son, Daniel.

"Are we going to scare her?" Daniel asked Frank.

"It's a surprise," Frank whispered and put his finger up to his lips.

"Should I go *Boo*?"

"No, Daniel," Dillon said. "It's not Halloween."

"Shush you two," Amy said. "Or you'll ruin it."

Frank could hear Wanda's boots coming up the steps. He glanced over and saw Ally and Ryan waiting in the kitchen for the right moment.

The front door opened.

"Surprise!" everyone shouted, appearing from their hiding places just as Wanda stepped into the living room.

"Oh my God," Wanda said with a genuine look of shock on her face. A banner hung on a wall wishing her both a HAPPY BIRTHDAY and HAPPY RETIREMENT.

"Thought it might be nice to celebrate them together." Frank walked up and gave his wife a kiss.

"You guys, you shouldn't have. Kill two birds with one stone, huh?"

Abbie, the family's golden retriever, rushed over to greet Wanda and received a welcoming pat on the head.

"Wait till you see the cake Gamma," Daniel said.

Wanda smiled at Dillon and Amy and picked Daniel up. "I can hardly wait," she told the boy.

"We couldn't fit all the candles on the cake 'cause you're so old."

"Daniel! Behave," Amy said, clearly embarrassed.

Wanda looked at her son. "Gee, Dillon. Does he remind you of someone?"

"Mom, I was never like that." Dillon put out his arms to take his son. "Come here, you little brat before you break Gamma's back."

Frank saw Wanda shaking her head and knew exactly what she was thinking.

Like father like son.

"What's this?" Wanda asked, reaching out to fondle Dillon's goatee.

"Amy thinks it looks cool," Dillon said with a proud smile.

"No, I don't," Amy piped in. "Stupid thing's scratchy."

Wanda turned as Ally and Ryan came over and gave their mom a big hug.

"This is such a wonderful surprise," Wanda said, unable to contain the tears. "How did you get here? I didn't see any cars."

"We parked behind the barn," Ryan said.

"Are you still driving a Trans Am?"

"Sure am."

"How have you been?' Wanda asked Ally. "Keeping busy?"

"Our hospital is sponsoring another animal rescue, so yes, we've been quite busy."

"How about I make everyone some drinks," Ryan volunteered and headed for the kitchen.

"If you'll excuse me for a moment, I'm going to change out of my uniform for the last time," Wanda said, and headed up the stairs.

Frank saw Amy staring at the small screen on her cell phone. She turned the device off, stuffed it in her jean pocket, and walked over to Frank.

"That was my dad sending me a text. He wanted me to tell you that he was sorry he and my mom couldn't make it today. He's still shook up about Jack's death."

"I heard. We were always kidding that Jack had nine lives like a cat. Tell your father it's okay, we understand."

Frank could hear the blender grinding in the kitchen, which meant that Ryan was making up a pitcher of margaritas.

"Can I go play outside on the swing?" Daniel asked his father.

"Only if you promise to stay out of trouble," Dillon said with a stern voice.

Daniel gave his father a perplexed look, like he had no idea what he was talking about.

"Just go."

Daniel ran into the kitchen.

"And don't wander off!"

But it was doubtful if Daniel was even listening as he dashed through the open door into the mudroom and bolted outside, slamming the screen door.

"A chip off the old block, eh?" Frank said.

"I wasn't that bad. Was I?" Dillon looked like he expected an answer but Frank just grinned.

Ryan came into the living room carrying a pitcher and placed it on the coffee table. Ally brought a tray of short-stemmed glasses with salt around the rims and put it next to the pitcher. Ryan was acting bartender and began pouring drinks.

Wanda came down the stairs, having changed into a blouse and a pair of jeans, and graciously took a glass. "Thank you, Ryan."

Dillon walked over to the flat screen TV mounted over the fireplace mantel. A program was on but the sound had been muted for the surprise party. "Isn't this that award-winning documentary that's been chronicling the restoration?"

"Looks like it."

A young filmmaker had come up with the idea and had produced over 30 separate two-hour long documentaries of how Earth was almost destroyed; segments about the asteroid belt and the deadly meteor showers, scientific studies of the tiny alien life forms and how they were able to transform insects into giant creatures; bleak footage of the military having to enforce Marshal Law; time progression of cities rebuilding their infrastructures, eventually sending up more communication satellites and restoring the Internet.

"Have you been downloading the series?" Frank asked.

"Yeah, I have most of them. I play the one with your interview all the time."

"How flattering."

"Daniel calls you The Bug Man."

"That so?"

"Strange how things panned out. The bugs dying off like that."

"Even the life forms couldn't alter the fact that insects, like everything else, have a life expectancy," Frank said. "Nothing lives forever."

"Do you think they got all of them?"

"The bugs or the life forms?"

"Both."

"Let's hope so."

Ally screamed from the kitchen.

"What the hell?" Frank placed his glass on the mantel and headed for the kitchen.

Wanda and Amy were also in the kitchen, standing by the counter where they had been preparing a platter of snack food.

"What's going on?" Frank asked as Dillon and Ryan joined him, gathering in the doorway.

Abbie crowded between their legs to see what was going on.

"Will you please tell Daniel to take that somewhere else," Ally pleaded.

The boy was holding a mason jar in his hands and was taunting Ally with it.

"Daniel, stop that!" Amy said.

Frank and Dillon stepped into the kitchen.

"What do you have there?" Frank asked.

Dillon knelt beside his son and looked through the glass. "Daniel's got himself a tarantula."

"I caught it outside."

"Did you know the scientific name for tarantulas is *Aphonepelma*?" Dillon said.

"How'd you know that?" Daniel asked.

"Frank told me when I was about your age."

"I can't believe you remembered," Frank said.

"Can I keep it?" Daniel asked his father.

"I've a better idea," Dillon said. "How about we take it outside and let it loose in the field across the road. That way it won't scare anyone and it can be with its friends. I don't think it's much fun being cooped up in a jar, do you?"

"I guess not."

"Come on. I know a special spot." Dillon stood and smiled. He let Daniel go first and followed his son through the mudroom and out the screen door.

Frank went back into the living room and retrieved his drink from the mantel.

Amy came out with the platter of snacks. Ally passed out paper plates while Ryan topped off everyone's glasses.

Frank put his arm around Wanda's shoulder, raised his glass in a toast, and gazed at her lovingly. "Happy birthday, dear. Here's to a new chapter in our lives."

Ryan, Ally, and Amy raised their glasses. "Happy birthday, Mom!"

Abbie joined in with a loud bark.

THE END

ACKNOWLEDGEMENTS

I would like to thank Gary Lucas and the wonderful people working with Severed Press that helped with this book. Special thanks to Nichola Meaburn for her editing and keen eye. It's truly amazing how folks we may never meet and who live in the most incredible places in the world can truly enrich our lives. And I would especially like to thank my daughter and faithful beta reader, Genene Griffiths Ortiz, for making this so much fun and sharing these bizarre and incredible journeys.

ABOUT THE AUTHOR

Gerry Griffiths lives in San Jose, California, with his family and their five rescue dogs and a cat. He is a Horror Writers Association member and has over thirty published short stories in various anthologies and magazines, as well as a short story collection entitled *Creatures*. He is also the author of *Silurid*, *The Beasts of Stoneclad Mountain*, and *Down From Beast Mountain* as well as *Death Crawlers* with the follow-up standalone novels, *Deep in the Jungle*, *The Next World*, and *Battleground Earth*, all published by Severed Press.

CHECK OUT OTHER GREAT HORROR NOVELS

BLACK FRIDAY
by Michael Hodges

Jared the kleptomaniac, Chike the unemployed IT guy, Patricia the shopaholic, and Jeff the meth dealer are trapped inside a Chicago supermall on Black Friday. Bridgefield Mall empties during a fire alarm, and most of the shoppers drive off into a strange mist surrounding the mall parking lot. They never return. Chike and his group try calling friends and family, but their smart phones won't work, not even Twitter. As the mist creeps closer, the mall lights flicker and surge. Bulbs shatter and spray glass into the air. Unsettling noises are heard from within the mist, as the meth dealer becomes unhinged and hunts the group within the mall. Cornered by the mist, and hunted from within, Chike and the survivors must fight for their lives while solving the mystery of what happened to Bridgefield Mall. Sometimes, a good sale just isn't worth it.

GRIMWEAVE
by Tim Curran

In the deepest, darkest jungles of Indochina, an ancient evil is waiting in a forgotten, primeval valley. It is patient, monstrous, and bloodthirsty. Perfectly adapted to its hot, steaming environment, it strikes silent and stealthy, it chosen prey: human. Now Michael Spiers, a Marine sniper, the only survivor of a previous encounter with the beast, is going after it again. Against his better judgement, he is made part of a Marine Force Recon team that will hunt it down and destroy it.

The hunters are about to become the hunted.

SEVEREDPRESS

f facebook.com/severedpress
🐦 twitter.com/severedpress

CHECK OUT OTHER GREAT HORROR NOVELS

DEATH CRAWLERS
by Gerry Griffiths

Worldwide, there are thought to be 8,000 species of centipede, of which, only 3,000 have been scientifically recorded. The venom of Scolopendra gigantea—the largest of the arthropod genus found in the Amazon rainforest—is so potent that it is fatal to small animals and toxic to humans. But when a cargo plane departs the Amazon region and crashes inside a national park in the United States, much larger and deadlier creatures escape the wreckage to roam wild, reproducing at an astounding rate. Entomologist, Frank Travis solicits small town sheriff Wanda Rafferty's help and together they investigate the crash site. But as a rash of gruesome deaths befalls the townsfolk of Prospect, Frank and Wanda will soon discover how vicious and cunning these new breed of predators can be. Meanwhile, Jake and Nora Carver, and another backpacking couple, are venturing up into the mountainous terrain of the park. If only they knew their fun-filled weekend is about to become a living nightmare.

THE PULLER
by Michael Hodges

Matt Kearns has two choices: fight or hide. The creature in the orchard took the rest. Three days ago, he arrived at his favorite place in the world, a remote shack in Michigan's Upper Peninsula. The plan was to mourn his father's death and figure out his life. Now he's fighting for it. An invisible creature has him trapped. Every time Matt tries to flee, he's dragged backwards by an unseen force. Alone and with no hope of rescue, Matt must escape the Puller's reach. But how do you free yourself from something you cannot see?

 SEVERED**PRESS**

 facebook.com/severedpress
 twitter.com/severedpress

CHECK OUT OTHER GREAT HORROR NOVELS

MONSTROSITY
by Tim Curran

The Food. It seeped from the ground, a living, gushing, teratogenic nightmare. It contaminated anything that ate it, causing nature to run wild with horrible mutations, creating massive monstrosities that roam the land destroying towns and cities, feeding on livestock and human beings and one another. Now Frank Bowman, an ordinary farmer with no military skills, must get his children to safety. And that will mean a trip through the contaminated zone of monsters, madmen, and The Food itself. Only a fool would attempt it. Or a man with a mission.

THE SQUIRMING
by Jack Hamlyn

You are their hosts

You are their food.

The parasites came out of nowhere, squirming horrors that enslaved the human race.They turned the population into mindless pack animals, psychotic cannibalistic hordes whose only purpose was to feed them.

Now with the human race teetering at the edge of extinction, extermination teams are fighting back, killing off the parasites and their voracious hosts. Taking them out one by one in violent, bloody encounters.

The future of mankind is at stake.

And time is running out.

www.ingramcontent.com/pod-product-compliance
Lightning Source LLC
Chambersburg PA
CBHW051954170626
46808CB00007B/2615